Devastated
The New Orleans Temptation Series

By:

Monica May

Copyright

First Original Edition, October 2014
Copyright © 2014 by Monica May
ISBN-13: 978-0-69-227869-7

ISBN-13: 978-0-69-227869-7

ACKNOWLEDGMENTS

Thanks to my husband and select friends (you know who you are) that read and approved of my smut. Without ya'll this book would not exist.

And a special thanks to an awesome editor. Editing by Kelly Hartigan (XterraWeb)
http://editing.xterraweb.com

******

Please be on the lookout for the remaining two books in the New Orleans Temptation Series by liking my Facebook page below.

https://www.facebook.com/pages/Monica-May

CONTENTS

Chapter 1

It has been a long busy week, but finally, Friday is here! My evening is spent like every Friday in the Chauvin household during football season, at the high school stadium, watching our son Blake play football.

Living in southeast Louisiana makes for a very hot August evening. After getting back from the game, it's time for a long shower to refresh. Before I make it to the bathroom, I see Grant has already fallen asleep on the sofa, as usual. My baby girl, Isabella, is up in her room watching preteen shows, while Blake is in his room playing video games.

I step out of the shower and look into the mirror. At thirty-nine, I am not overweight, but could stand to lose a few pounds. I am far from fit. I have to come up with a plan to get into shape and get back down to my pre-pregnancy weight of sixteen years ago. I can do it if I put my mind to it; all I need is a plan. But what is the plan? I have it! I'm going to text Zoe. She's in her late forties and is in better shape than I am at thirty-nine.

Now that I am done with my after-shower moisturizing routine, I flop down on the sofa beside my sleeping Grant, with a large glass of wine. I know he works hard all day in the hot sun, but really, it is 9:30! He is asleep as soon as his ass hits the sofa. Seeing him asleep makes me wonder where the days of being all over each other have gone. I look at his weathered face, from years of working out in the elements, and he is still handsome. He has a strong jaw line, scruffy five-o'clock shadow, and the most beautiful black eyelashes.

Watching him sleep brings me back into the past. We met the summer after I graduated from high school. I was 18, and he was 21. We both fell in love hard and fast. I saw what I wanted, and I took it. Grant has told me that's what drew him to me. He likes a woman who knows how to take charge.!

We had common friends, but did not know each other. A usual Friday night back then was far different from today. Those Fridays were spent getting ready with my girlfriends—putting on makeup, fixing our hair, crazy singing, and dancing. After two hours of gussying up, we were ready to go out to the club for a night filled with drinking and dancing. Back in the nineties, Louisiana's drinking age was only eighteen, and we loved it.

Once we made it to the club, I saw a friend, Jodi, from high school. She introduced us to the group of people she was hanging out with. That's when I saw him. I was instantly drawn to him, from the moment I laid eyes on him. I wanted to get to know him, dance with him, and talk to him. Unfortunately, he was there with someone else. She was cute, but they didn't appear to want to be there together. She had a permanent scowl on her face, and they were sitting so far away from each other, they couldn't touch each other if they wanted to.

After our brief hello, we continued to the bar. We hung out at the bar for a while ordering drinks, checking out who was there, playing who's hot and who's not. But I couldn't keep my eyes off him. There was something about him that was pulling me to him. Jodi caught me staring.

"Grant, his name is Grant. By the way, no one likes his girlfriend, so feel free to cause a stir. She's a bitch, and he is looking for a reason to drop her."

I looked across the club to see him sitting on a stool by himself now as his girlfriend Mandy walked away from him angrily. I finished the drink in my hand and took a fresh one from Jodi. "He is about to find a reason!" With a wink, I was off to see if he was interested in dropping her.

I crossed the club with my eyes zeroed in on my target. When I saw he's watching me saunter over to him, I put a little extra swing in my hips. I approached him where he sat on a stool, "Come dance with me, handsome." He looked me up and down, and I stood there in front of him and let him take me in.

Country was hot at the time, and I was dressed to the nines in western wear. His eyebrows rose when he saw my big curly nineties hair that hung over my shoulders and fell below my elbows. His gaze continued down to my bright mauve-colored lipstick. His beautiful green eyes widened when he saw my sleeveless plaid button-down shirt with the buttons undone far enough to see how full my breasts are.

His attention went down to my flat stomach, which was exposed by my tied-off Daisy Duke styled shirt and down to my short shorts that were almost too short. If I had not been wearing a thong, my panties would have certainly hung out the bottom. He looked me over thoroughly from head to toe, even taking in my very toned and tanned legs before finally stopping on my cowboy boots. I had to admit I was pretty hot. Oh, where had the time and that body gone?

I cleared my throat to help him regain focus on what I

told him to do. When he brought his eyes back up to my face, I repeated myself. "Come dance with me, handsome." He smiled a very sexy smile. He had perfectly straight white teeth, strong muscular arms, and hair so dark brown it was almost black. He looked rugged in the hot fireman way with the sexiest legs I had ever seen on a man in my life.

"I am sorry; I don't dance."

I yelled over the music. "You do now; let's go!" I grabbed him by the hand, pulling him off the stool. I had him up against my body dancing the rest of the night. In the last twenty-one years, I don't think we have spent a weekend apart since that night.

Six months later, we were engaged. We could not stand to be apart. Our bodies needed each other constantly. Our first time together was so HOT, in more ways than one. It was July in south Louisiana, and it was eighty-two degrees with thick humid air. After a night of dancing and partying with friends, Grant drove us to the end of the bayou. From this view, you could see the city lights of New Orleans over the water. The only sounds heard was the lapping of the water as trawl boats passed in the distance, frogs, and crickets. He turned onto a Cypress-tree-lined road that lead to the parking lot near the dock. My heart was beating so hard it was pounding in my ears. I wanted him so badly.

He turned off the lights and the engine to avoid waking the neighbors living in the houseboats nearby. Turning to me, he gave me his oh-so-sexy smile. I knew the time was right for us; I loved him so much it hurt to be without him. Reaching over the seat, his hand was in the back of my hair pulling my face to his. He kissed me with so much lust and desire. I was not a virgin, but I had only had one other lover, and I was a bit nervous. Grant was a few years older than me and so damn manly compared to the boy I dated back in high school. I was unsure if I would know what to do with him.

We kissed deeply for what seemed like hours. He was trying to be a gentleman, but I couldn't take it any longer. I needed him. I opened my eyes to see his green eyes staring back at me with the same lust and desire I felt in between my legs.

"I need you inside of me, Grant." He was always so sweet, such a southern gentleman, making sure I knew he would wait if I wasn't ready. "Are you sure you are ready? I will wait for you, how ever long it takes for you to be ready."

I gave him a sexy smile. "Fuck me now!"

"Whatever you say, Bossy Girl." That had been his nickname for me ever since I pulled him off the bar stool and made him dance with me. Slowly unbuttoning my shirt, he pushed it over my shoulders, and I felt goose bumps appear everywhere his fingers trailed. I let out a moan as he licked a line of sweat dripping down the middle of my breasts to my navel. It felt so good to have his tongue on my skin. I lifted my body off the seat allowing his hands to unsnap my bra. My breasts were now at his full disposal. I watched his fingers as he rolled my nipple in between his thumb and index finger. This was something I had never felt before, and it's a divine pleasurable pain. At that moment, I knew it was going to be beyond anything I had ever experienced, especially considering I had only had sex missionary style in a twin bed. When I said missionary only, I meant it—no other position, no other touching, just kissing, in and out, in and out, that's it! Sad I knew, but it was the truth.

Needless to say, this was beyond anything I could have imagined. The feeling of him twisting my nipple was so intense; it sent a direct line of pleasure right to my pussy. He hit the button on the seat and pushed it all the way back, flat onto the back seat, allowing him room to move into my seat and hover over me. Eyes locked on mine, his tongue was now on my bare nipple, pulling it into his mouth and repeating the process with the other nipple. That's all it took for me to be gone, gone to a place I had never visited before. He was in full control, which was different from our relationship; Grant allowed me to control everything else, but this I will allow him to control—he was oh so good at it.

His large hands moved down to the button on my shorts, undoing them quickly. With a steady pull, my shorts and panties were down and off my sweat-covered body. I was now completely naked in the front seat of his car. At that time in my life, this was the most erotic thing I had ever done. We had no concern for the outside world. We should have been more concerned with someone seeing us or hearing us, but we didn't care about anything but what we were feeling.

I pulled his shirt over his head to see his chiseled chest, covered in a soft blanket of dark hair. With a moan, I ran my hand up and down his chest with a moan.

"I'm going to eat your beautiful pussy, Shelby. I have

wanted to do this since the day I saw you in those short shorts," he said as he brushed his thumb over my clit. "I need to taste you; you want me to taste you, don't you?" I looked at him and blushed. I had never had this done to me before. I had heard about it, but had never experienced it. He smirked at me. "Tell me you have been licked here before?"

"No, never, I want you to be the first and the last."

"You will love it. I am the best," he said with confidence. Oh, did I love it. His tongue slid in between my folds to find me soaked. "You taste so sweet, Bossy Girl." His warm breath flowed in between my legs, giving me goose bumps again as he spoke.

My hips naturally lifted to him as his fingers pumped in and out of me steadily, while he slowly licked my clit and pulled it into his mouth. He licked me like he couldn't get enough. The combination of the two was breathtaking. Between the slow sensual licks and an occasional suck of my clit, I was about to come undone. I started to feel pressure build from within my soul. He didn't let up as he sensed I was close.

"Come for me; let go, feel it. Go ahead, Bossy Girl, I am telling you to come for me now." I did as he said on command, all over his face. I felt the relief of my most intense orgasm to date cream right out of me. "Did you like being fucked with my mouth?"

"Oh God, I loved it; promise you will never stop doing that to me. Ever."

"Never, Bossy Girl, I will never stop doing this to you. Even when you are old and gray, I will keep licking you."

We both laughed only stopping when he continued to

gently lap at my swollen lips while unbuttoning his pants. Within seconds, his beautiful cock was free, standing at attention. I watched as he rolled a condom down his long erection. I wanted to feel his length inside me.

He rubbed the head of his dick up and down my soaking wet pussy. It felt so good. Staring into my eyes, he gently yet firmly pushed into me. My back arched off the seat to meet him. I couldn't believe how different this felt from anything I had experienced in the past. He's so hard and long, my missing puzzle piece. The way he moved inside of me was ecstasy. I knew at that moment we were made for each other. I was going to keep him for a lifetime.

I vaguely heard Grant moan something about me being wet and tight. But I was in a daze, too consumed with the feeling of him moving within me, rocking my hips forward to allow him to go deeper with each thrust. His mouth came down to my nipple, and his sucking almost threw me over the edge again. I was barely hanging on when his thrusting increased, and we both came with such force I was sure this was a onetime thing that would never be repeated. Boy, was I wrong. I had no idea how our screams of pleasure didn't wake the neighbors nearby.

We lay clinging to each other as we caught our breath. He was still slowly and gently pumping in and out of me. Had the mosquitoes not been coming in the open window and biting us, we might still be lying in that spot this very day.

Chapter 2

"Mom … Mom". The sound of my son calling me as he comes down the stairs brings me back to the current time. He sits next to me, sitting on top of his father's legs that are taking up the entire sofa at the moment. He's my baby boy, and now that he is in high school, I am having a hard time coming to grips with the fact that he is going to leave me for college soon. He tells me he is getting tired, has turned his game off, and came to kiss me goodnight. He also informs me that Isabella is knocked out in her bed with the light and TV on, so he kindly shut it all off for her.

While I am listening to all his information, I start to text Zoe about what she does to stay fit. Blake continues to chat about what's going on at school. He loves to extend going to bed, no matter how tired he is. I usually let him, especially when it's not a school night. I take all the information he is willing to give because before I know it, he will be off to college.

Zoe has sent me a picture of the yoga DVD she uses. I can't believe she doesn't lift weights and only does yoga! I mean, really, how hard can yoga be? I will have to look this up tomorrow and give it a try.

My attention is turned back to my son. He is asking me questions about his deceased grandfather. He has always been such a deep-thinking child. Our conversation finds its way to his grandfather's last visit to our home. I grab my husband's phone from the bar above my head to find a picture I believe we took at that visit.

As I hit the photo app, all of the blood drains from my face. I am frozen; I can't think, can't move. I am not sure if I am even breathing. Blake breaks me from my trance. "Mom, are you okay? You look like you saw a ghost!" I hear him say it, but it sounds like he's a million miles away. I do my best to get it together.

"It's time for bed. I don't feel well, and I have to run to the restroom. The picture is not where I thought it was, son; I will look on the computer for you tomorrow."

After a kiss on my cheek, he says, "Hope you feel better, Mom!" I love that boy so much.

OMG, OMG, OMG is all I can say in my head as I run to the bathroom and lock the door behind me, not that anyone is coming after me. Grant is dead to the world on the sofa. He has no clue I picked up his phone only to find pictures of him with his pants down. Literally with his pants down, and his hands around his erection! There are three photos in different stages of an erection, going from firm to OMG big.

I know I had a very big glass of wine; am I really seeing this? Is this my imagination? As I rub my eyes, I exit the screen then go back to the app just to make sure. Yep, this is really happening to me!

I am pissed. I know those pictures were not sent to me. I start to thumb through texts to see who he sent these to. There are no texts that include these pictures. I storm though the living room to the computer room and pull up our phone bill on the computer. The phone bill is pretty current showing the text I just sent to Zoe thirty minutes ago. I see no numbers from his phone that I don't recognize. What the hell?

I'm not sure what woke Grant up, but he comes into the room where I'm searching the computer. With one look at my face, he knows something is terribly wrong.

"Hey, what's going on? What's wrong with you?" I throw his phone at him, and with a voice I do not recognize as my own, I yell, "This is what's fucking wrong!"

He catches the phone just before it hits the ground. Looking at the screen, his shoulders slump and a look of shame crosses his face. I start to get out of the chair to get past him. I can't bear to be in the same room with him at this moment. He grabs my arm on my way out the door. "I can explain; it's not what it looks like."

"Really? You mean to tell me this is not a picture of you jacking off and sending it to someone other than me? You must be out of your fucking mind if you think I am falling for that shit." And quite frankly, he knows me better than to think I would. With a mad-as-hell face, I try to hide my pain. "So, tell me what it is, because it sure as hell looks as if you are cheating on me, sexting your girlfriend."

"I have never cheated on you." The response flies out of his mouth. At this moment, there is no way my brain will compute this.

I try to shrug my arm out of his grip. He wants to explain, but I don't want to hear it. I need to get away, get out of this house. My kids have gone to bed, and I don't know how to have this conversation right now. We have never had issues in our marriage, ever. We don't typically argue, fight, scream, or yell. If we disagree, we usually talk it out and come to a compromise. I am out of my element, and as a control freak, I can't deal with it. I have to run. I have to have a plan, a thought process. I look at him with eyes of daggers, "Let my arm go, NOW."

"We have to talk about this; you have to let me explain."

"I don't want to hear it." I grab my purse and storm out the door.

I have no clue where I am going; my brain is not working properly. I can barely see past the rage, hurt, and anger I feel. I drive until I get to the end of the road. I park my car at the river and have a total meltdown alone in my car, alongside the banks of the breathtaking Tchefuncte River under massive one-hundred-year-old oak trees. I'm now crying uncontrollably—something I have never done. I can handle this, right? I don't know how to handle this. This is not us, this is not our marriage, that is what I keep telling myself.

When I pulled out of our driveway, I had turned off the tracking on my phone. I didn't want him to find me. Not that he would even look, but just in case. I can't bear to hear his voice right now. How could he? How could he do this to me, to us, to our family? Why? Why did he do this? All these questions are coming to my mind, and I don't have an answer for one of them. Not one!

We don't argue over anything but money! We have sex at least three times a week. We do everything together except for our jobs. Where in the hell did he have the time for this? How could I not know? I am done asking myself questions I don't have answers for. Just as that thought crosses my mind, my phone starts beeping.

Chapter 3

Grant:
12:35 a.m.
Where r u?
I am worried about u
U should not be driving
U had too much wine
I am SO sorry let me explain

Shelby:
12:37 a.m.
Don't act all worried when u could hv cared less when u were pulling ur dick out & texting it to someone OTHER than me

Grant:
12:38 a.m.
It's not what it looks like
Call me so I can explain
Or come home so we can talk

Shelby:
12:38 a.m.
Right now I cant stand the thought of seeing ur face r hearing your voice

This is all I am gonna gv u so start texting

Grant:
12:39 a.m.
1st I am SO SORRY

Shelby:
12:39 a.m.
Yea sorry I found out?

Grant:
12:40 a.m.
Please let me explain!
I am sorry I did it
Its not your fault its mine
I take responsibility
I was reading msg boards on porn
sites & started commenting
It got out of hand
That site brought me to an app that shows
picture for 3 sec
It turned into show me yours & I'll show u mine

Shelby:
12:45 a.m.
What r u fucking 12?
They all look the same u ass
Am I not enough 4 u?
I don't understand the need?
Its not like we don't do it 3 times a week!

What else do u want frm me?

Grant:
12:47 a.m.
Its not u & I am an ass
I LOVE U
I don't ever want to be w/out u
Please I am so sorry it just got out of control
I promise it wont happen again

12:50 a.m.
R u there?

1:05 a.m.
R u ok?

Shelby:
1:10 a.m.
I honestly dont know how to respond to this
We get along
Nothing in our relationship has changed that I know of?
Has it?

Grant:
1:12 a.m.
No nothing has changed I am an idiot
I am sorry
I love u so much please come home

Shelby
1:14 a.m.
I will be home when I get there
Turning my phone off

"Grant"

I can't believe I'm this stupid! What have I done? I knew I shouldn't have gotten on that site and hit that chat button. It started off with me trying to find new things to talk Shelby into. But I knew she would never let me tie her up or spank her. She is so strong-minded, and that is one of the reasons I fell in love with her. But that strong will is also her vice at times. She makes up her mind before she even tries anything. I wish I could have tried to open her mind.

I knew it was wrong the entire time. But it was so damn exciting! So erotic! It wasn't the person that made it sexy. It was what we were talking about, and what we were sending to each other.

Not to mention, I am sure it was all a lie. I lied about my name, my age, and my marital status. I never sent anyone a picture of my face. Damn it, I knew this was bad, but I just couldn't stop myself. I love Shelby so much, but our sex life has been a bit boring for sometime now. I know that's a piss-poor excuse, but it's a fact. I need to talk to her. I need to explain to her I never cheated. I am sure that won't help much, but we have to talk.

What am I going to tell her that doesn't make it feel like it's her fault? I am just going to take all the blame, call myself a piece of shit, and beg for her forgiveness. I will tell her I will do ANYTHING she wants me to do to get through this. I have to admit, I am glad she found them. It was starting to get way out of control.

At first, it was just flirty women who would ask, "You want to see my tits?" or "I would love for you to see a picture of my wet pussy. Do you want to see it?" Really, that's how crazy these chat sites are. Then someone asked me to send her a picture of my dick getting hard after she had sent a picture of her dripping wet pussy. So I did it. Why, I'm still not sure, but it was exciting to take a picture of my hard cock and send it.

I guess I really need to question my motives and myself before Shelby gets back home. God, I hope she comes back home tonight. I'm really worried about her. She is so upset. She may get into a wreck or something. I was knocked out on the sofa, but I see her empty glass of wine. I am sure she had her typical large glass. Damn it, why didn't I stop her from driving off?

Why did I do this? Was it exciting because it was a stranger? Because it wasn't Shelby? No, it was the act that was exciting. I would love for Shelby to send me pictures from work of her wet pussy and tell me she is thinking of me and thinking of fucking me. That would be so much fun and different from our normal vanilla sex life. So why in the hell did I not tell her that? Why did I not ask her to try sexting with me?

That question has an easy answer—she would never do such a thing. In a way, I understand her thinking; she thinks she has to be all proper and motherly all the time.

She never wants to try anything new or different. Maybe I should have pushed her harder to try new stuff with me? I should have, I really should have, done that before doing what I did. I have to fix this. I can't live my life without Shelby. I am mentally willing her to walk through that door safe, or simply turn her phone back on.

I am sitting at the table staring at the phone with my head in my hands. I ask God to help me. I shouldn't ask because I don't even go to church with Shelby and the kids. But I have to; I need her back. God, I promise to be better to Shelby than I ever have; please give me one chance to make it up to her. Please, God, please keep her safe until she gets home. There is nothing left for me to do but wait. I sit and stare at the phone while I wait. It's now 3:00 a.m.! She has been gone for almost three hours. My phone beeps—it's Shelby!

Chapter 4

"Shelby"

At some point, I need to bring myself to drive home. I'm completely devastated! He says he did not cheat on me, but it most certainly feels like it. I have sat on the bank of the river for hours watching boats go by in the still of the night. I wish I could go with them and get the hell out of here to go anywhere else but here. Is that something I could do, just leave? Leave my kids, my family, my home, and my job? My husband of almost twenty motherfucking years?

It makes me angry; I'm mad as hell. I have given him everything I have. I gave Grant my body when it was perfect all those years before we had kids. My body was changed forever by having HIS children. My boobs are nowhere near where they were when I was nineteen, and my butt is larger than it used to be. And, of course, my stomach is far from tight or flat after two kids. I never took time for myself, and didn't really try to get back into shape because I was too busy being a mother. Was I the problem? Was he no longer attracted to me?

These thoughts go through my mind while I look up at the oak trees that must hold so many secrets.

Who in the hell does he think he is? Does he think he is as attractive as the day I met him? I mean, really, he's still a very nice-looking man, but neither of us look nineteen anymore.

Then it came to me. I am not a quitter! I am a fighter

who never loses what she fights for. This is not about my body or me. If he had an issue or felt neglected, he needed to communicate that to me, not go texting his dick to random people on some stupid app.

It's about 3:00 a.m. when I pull into the driveway. I am disappointed when he doesn't rush out of the house to greet me. Actually, truth be told, I am pissed that he does not come out. Did he just fall asleep like it's no big deal? Okay, Shelby, calm yourself down. You have to be reasonable, that's what I keep telling myself, but it's tough to do.

I walk around the side of the house to peak in the back blinds and see if I can see him. I am shocked when I see him staring at his phone on the table, willing it to ring, waiting to hear from me. He couldn't leave the kids home alone in the middle of the night, so he was stranded here waiting on my word. I hate to admit it, but it makes me feel better to see the pain on his face. In the way he's holding his body, I know I should not be glad, but my heart hurts so much right now I want him to hurt too.

I turn my phone back on and start to text him.

Shelby:
3:12 a.m.
I dont know how we get past this

Grant:
3:12 a.m.
Thank god u r ok
I hv been so worried
I am SO SORRY

PLEASE COME HOME

Shelby:
3:15 a.m.
I am home.

He finally finds me sitting outside under the back patio. We talk for a long time about what has happened and what we're going to do about it. The bottom line is he has always been a porn man, and I never understood it or cared to. He has always wanted something more exciting than what we were doing. He said it started with him looking for new things for us to do. "I knew you would never try any of the stuff I saw online."

Being so young when we got together, I let him lead us in the bedroom, but I wouldn't allow certain things that made me uncomfortable. Watching porn was one of them. I had no desire to see it.

I was not mature enough at the time to try anything but plain vanilla, considering the things he did to me were above and beyond what I had done before him. I assumed we were doing more than plain old vanilla. Then the kids came. I have to admit I was even less tolerable of anything new after that. I was either too tired or too stressed to stay awake or care. We had sex once during the week and twice on the weekends. We both always have orgasms and they were usually at the same time. Good, right? So I thought! What else did he want?

A day or two goes by with me only speaking to Grant when necessary. I am just too hurt. I had explained to him exactly this, "I have given you my heart and my soul for twenty-one years. You have sliced my chest open, ripped my heart out, and stomped on it! You have to give me time to put my heart back together. If you don't like the silent treatment or my attitude, too fucking bad, deal with it."

Believe it or not, he understood that. He knew me too well; he knew it would only take me a few days to come up with a plan. That's just how I work; I'm a fixer. Everything can be fixed, if you have a plan to fix it. That's what I needed. But how? What was going to be the plan? How in God's name could I ever compete with that stuff he sees on TV? It's all a bunch of nonsense! No one really does that kind of stuff. Do they?

The plan hit me like a ton of bricks! Find out if anyone is really doing the stuff I have refused to believe was real-life stuff. The start of my plan was to read that book everyone was gabbing about—that one book with the tie on it.

I was never a reader. Grant had mentioned this book to me about a month before what I now call the "cyber incident." He said it made his coworker's wife so hot she gave it to him on the kitchen table after putting the kids to bed. Right there on the table! Was he for real? I ignored his suggestion back then because I thought his co-worker was full of shit. Why would I read porn? After college, I never read anything but magazines and the Internet.

Here goes nothing! I don't tell Grant about my plan. I still have enough pain in me to want him to feel the same misery. I want him to see my sad soul, to know my heart has been ripped into a thousand pieces. I want him to feel my anxiety. I am too strong for this shit. I don't quit and I don't panic.

This is all a new world to me. I don't break down, I don't cry, and I don't whine. I just get up, dust off, and keep moving. That's how I'm built. This is how we are built as a couple. I didn't have a panic attack when we lost our entire home to Hurricane Katrina eight years ago.

We lost everything we owned. The only things we had were each other, the kids, and the clothes we had packed in the car when we left. Grant and I broke down for literally thirty seconds when we drove up to our flood-ravished home. Thirty seconds is all we allowed, then we decided to deal with it. We were not the only people in the New Orleans area that were devastated by this storm, so why would we think we were special enough to bellyache about it.

We taught the kids to feel lucky that all of their family was safe. The house and the stuff in it was just "stuff." None of the stuff is important; family is the most important thing, and we were all together. My siblings, my parents, my grandparents, and Grant's family lost everything also. It was a rough go for a while, but we did it without moaning and groaning about it.

We simply moved from south of New Orleans to north of Lake Pontchartrain. That was the plan, the plan that let us sleep at night. We were no longer close enough to be inundated with floodwaters if another storm hit, but we were still close enough to keep our jobs and visit the family members that didn't move. That's what we did. This should be a cakewalk.

Chapter 5

I started to read. WOW was all I could say after reading the first book. I read it in less than a week, and I have to admit, while the book intrigued me, I still thought, *This is fantasy stuff, right? Real people don't do this, do they?* Then I read book two, then book three. While I still thought it was a fantasy, I was hooked. I was introduced to thoughts that were never in the realm of my imagination. And I liked it. However, I was not ready to admit this to Grant yet.

I kept downloading more books. I looked for books without millionaires to help me relate to real people. During this time, Grant and I had more conversations as to what drove him to do what he did. I was beginning to feel more acceptance for what had transpired, especially since I knew I was now hooked on porn myself. But my addiction was paper porn, not video porn. It was a video all right, a video in my head, but there was no tape to watch.

Meanwhile, I started my high-protein-low-to-no-carb diet. That was as soon as I was able to hold food down after the "cyber incident." It has only been about two weeks since then, but I have already lost six pounds. I also started Zoe's yoga DVD! This girl is nuts. This is not yoga; this is torture. If you have never tried yoga, don't even think for one second that it is easy! Easy is one thing yoga is not, but I was determined, so I kept at it.

In only two weeks and a lot of communication, I learned we were both to blame. Grant's part was not communicating his needs to me. My part was not trusting him enough to try new things.

It is another Friday night after a high school football game. It's a little different now though. Grant is much more attentive. He is actually awake on the sofa socializing with the kids and I until it is time for them to go to bed.

I have had my typical large glass of wine. I have used my wine in the past to help unwind from the week at work. Now, I am using it to cope, using it to get through each day, to dull the pain. Even though I have a better understanding, it didn't make it hurt any less. I am trying to break myself away from this pity party. I keep asking myself who in the heck do I think I am boohooing over this. He never slept with anyone.

I convinced myself it's simply an extension of porn. That's the only way I can deal with it. It doesn't matter if it's the right way. It's the way it has to be in order to live the rest of my life married to this man.

I can no longer harbor hate. I have to try and get over it. I have to try to trust him again, and love him again. And by that, I mean make love to him again. He has not dared ask for it. But I know him, I know he is waiting on me to be ready. I have always let him be in charge. But I now know one of his complaints was I never initiated sex.

Both kids are busy entertaining friends upstairs. I allowed each to have one friend sleep over tonight. So with no one looking over my shoulder, here goes, part two of "Operation Save My Marriage." While Grant is in the shower, I check out a few lingerie websites on my kindle. Amazed at how cheap this stuff is, I order about 150 dollars' worth of sexy wear. Now, what should I do while I wait for my shipment?

It suddenly comes to me, a scene from one of my smut books. Bath time! How simple, still kind of vanilla, but I can't remember a time when we have taken a bath together. Maybe once before Blake was born?

First thing Saturday morning, I get dressed and feed the kids and their friends. I start some light cleaning until the other parents pick up their kids. Isabella worms her way into going home with her friend so she can sleep there for the night. Blake hears she is sleeping out and asks if he can go home with his friend. With that turn of events, we are now home alone for the night.

I grab my purse and head out the door for the bath store and the usual Saturday grocery shopping. I have never been a bath person, always preferring showers. However, after some heavy smut reading, I think we have been missing out.

As soon as I open the door to the bath store, a very perky twenty-something-year-old girl with an apron on asks me if she can give me a tote for all my purchases. She hands me the bag and follows me around the store asking if she can help me. I accept her help; I don't know where anything is in this store. She points me in the direction of the bubble bath, matching massage oils, and lotion.

These are perfect items for my plan on a perfect night without the kids. If the kids were home, I would have to wait until they fell asleep or risk explaining why mom and dad are both in the bathroom at the same time for so long. As my thoughts drift while standing in line, another salesperson talks me into buying candles. She says, "You can't have a nice bubble bath without candles." The store is packed; there is a sale on everything. Waiting in line, I remember Grant once or twice mentioning how he would love to buy massage oil. Another one of his suggestions I totally ignored. He is going to be floored!

When I get home, Grant is still outside doing yard work and cleaning up from cutting the grass. After the groceries are put away, I start to clean the tub. It's very dusty from lack of use. When that's complete, I sit down to rest. Pulling out my Kindle, I put my feet up on the ottoman and read a few chapters of my latest book until Grant yells from the back door for a glass of water. I turn my Kindle off; I have wasted enough time resting.

As I go to the back door with his water, I am caught off guard when I notice how sexy he looks out there. How did I miss that for the last few years? He is standing over the pool skimming the grass out of it. No shirt, just a pair of athletic shorts hung low on his hips. Sweat glistens over his entire body. The muscles in his arms flex with every swipe of the pool skimmer. Have I been dead for years? Moving through life making sure my kids are fed, clean, smart, respectful, and well rounded, I have neglected myself and our marriage. As I watch him through the glass, I feel throbbing between my legs.

I bring him his water and tell him I am not cooking tonight; we are going to go out for dinner. As I walk away, he asks, "Where are we going to eat?"

I yell over the pool, "Dinner is your choice. I have a

surprise for dessert!" He lowers his head so I can see his wide eyes over his sunglasses. For the first time in a long time, I see his sexy smile. I giggle and look at him before I shut the door. "Hurry your ass up because I am starving." With a wink, I am gone to shower and get ready for dinner.

We have dinner at a local seafood restaurant since we were both craving fresh red fish. He gets his fish fried and topped with a heavy crawfish cream sauce. It looks delicious, but that does not fit into my diet. I order grilled red fish topped with lemon wine sauce with lump crabmeat. We have a nice conversation as we talk about the events of the week, the kids, and what's going on with each other's job.

Grant has become a superintendent for the construction company he has worked for since we met. The new position has really stressed him out, and I never bother to ask him how things are going at work. Our time is usually monopolized with talk of the kids. Now that I think about it, the kids are usually breathing down our necks constantly. I love them, but at the moment, I don't miss them at all.

After dinner is done, we head home.
Pulling into the driveway, he asks if I would let him in on what's for dessert? The suspense is killing him. "Lets go relax on the sofa with a glass of wine, and I will let you in on the secret when we're done."

We sit on the sofa with my feet in his lap and chat about the past and the fun we used to have in our younger years. I finish my wine first and start to drink out of his glass. I am anxious to get to the dessert as well.

Chapter 6

I get up from the sofa once I've drained the rest of Grant's wine from his glass. "Give me five minutes, then meet me in the bathroom."

I rush off to get everything set up. I have OCD, so I already have all my new purchases in the bathroom closet. I start to pull it out as I fill the tub. When I add the blackberry vanilla bubble bath to the water, the scent fills the entire room.

That saleslady pointed me in the right direction when I told her I needed a scent that was not too girly. This smell is very sensual. I should have guessed that since the name on the bottle reads, "Sensual Aromatherapy." She also paired the bubble bath with a pecan waffle candle that is to die for. I had already put the lighter in my bag, and the candles are now taken care of. I'm all done with the setup.

With one minute left, I toss my clothes into the laundry basket. Before I slip into the hot water, I hit my music app to play love songs from the nineties. Perfect. The room is absolutely perfect. This is straight from a page in one of my books. All I need is my man to walk in the door. Right on cue, the door swings open. Grant stands there in awe of me covered only in bubbles waiting for him in the candle-lit room.

He strides across the room shucking off his clothes as he heads to the tub. He slowly steps in as I lean forward to allow him room to slip in behind me. We say nothing, feeling the want and desire in the air. He wraps his now slick arms around me. "I love you so much; do you know that?" I shake my head yes while he grabs my conveniently placed bath sponge and pours the matching liquid soap into it. "This shit smells good. When did you get all this stuff?"

"Don't you worry about my secrets; you just enjoy the outcome."

"You know, we have not taken a bath together in quite some time." This is the information I recalled while standing in line at the bath store. It makes me sad that he remembers that as well. *Shelby, try to shake off the sad. This is a new effort; turn a new leaf.* I feel something turning all right; I feel Grant's dick start to rise and press into my back. A smile crosses my face. My plan is working.

He washes my shoulders as he brings the soap-filled sponge across my breasts, paying close attention to my nipples that are now erect and begging for attention. He moves the silky, yet rough, sponge in circles with very little pressure over one nipple. The light touch is driving me crazy for more. It feels good, but the need for more is building between my legs. He switches over to the other nipple! That's my man—giving equal attention to each nipple. I'm not sure how much longer I can hold out without coming.

I sit up, turn to him, and wrap my legs around his waist. I reach over for the massage oil. I start to twist the top as he watches with excitement. "Is that what I think it is? Is that massage oil?" My smile answers his question as I pour a long dramatic stream into my left hand.

Grant holds his hand out to me, and I fill his palm as well. Within seconds, we are rubbing each other down and panting. We start at each other's shoulders, move slowly down each other's arms, and massage hands and fingers. I would have never guessed this would make my blood boil the way it is right now. His large fingers are massaging each of my fingers individually, and it's so suggestive. With his fingers in an O-shape, he pulls each of my fingers through his.

That is the feeling I want; I want him in me. But I have to be patient and let this whole seduction scene play out. Grant brings me out of my thoughts by dropping my hands in the warm water and moving his to my thighs.

I follow suit with my hands disappearing under the bubbles to find Grant's erection. I have not felt Grant this large in years. I wrap my hands around his shaft. With already oiled hands, I start to firmly guide my fingers up and down his cock. To my surprise, it feels good to me— good to please him, and good to know that I know what I am doing. I have learned more valuable information in the last two weeks of reading smut than I had in four years of college.

Using my newfound information, I lower my other hand to cup his balls. His face goes rigid and I can see he has started to panic. I guess the unknown is scary for everyone. It only takes a few careful firm tugs of his balls for him to realize it feels good. "Shelby, if you do that much longer, I am going to come right here!"

Leaning over to his ear, in the sexiest voice I have, I whisper, "That's the plan, sweetheart!"

With that, he lets go, letting me make him feel good, letting my hands take him to heaven and back. I continue to move my hand up and down his cock, slowly adding pressure as I reach the base and letting up on the pressure when I come up to the head. With some gentle tugs of his balls, Grant's head drops back. He calls my name with such lust, I almost come with him. I pump him until he begs me to stop.

Grant grasps my shoulders pulling me to him and kissing me deeply. His tongue invades my mouth with such determination. His strong forceful tongue circles mine as he sucks my tongue into his mouth like he is sucking a Popsicle. My pussy is now up against his cock, which to my amazement is hard again. I can't even recall the last time this happened this quickly. I am in delightful shock.

He puts his large hands under my ass, lifting me onto his hard cock. As he lets me down onto himself, he lowers a hand onto my nipple and he starts to twist it. He twists a steady, firm, constant twist as I dig my heels into the tub starting to ride him. In this squatted position, I have great leverage to move up and down his length. Once I hit the base, I rub my clit onto him in circles. My orgasm is close. I continue the same movements with increased pressure while Grant does the same to my nipple. "I am going to come, please don't stop, please don't let up, I need you, I need you to want me!" I explode into a million pieces. At the same time, Grant finds his release again, and I feel him pumping inside of me.

We are both limp trying to catch our breath. I think we have died and gone to heaven. It's been so long since each of us has put so much effort into making the other come. This is a trend we should continue. Grant picks me up out of the tub, sets me on my feet, and dries me off with such care and tenderness.

Chapter 7

We go to bed together without another word, just lying in each other's arms, so close, so loving. It is almost as if our issues have been washed away in the bathtub.

Boy, was I ever wrong! In the early morning hours, I wake in horror. I think I may be having a panic attack. I have never had one in my life. I would have told you they don't exist, and people make that shit up. But, oh my Lord, I feel as if I can't breathe. I am gasping for air; my heart is about to beat out of my chest, and I am sweating like a pig.

Grant wakes and sees the panic on my face, "What's the matter, are you okay?"

"I don't know? I don't know what's happening? I can barely breathe. My heart is beating so fast. I just need to calm down and take some long slow breaths." After about twenty minutes of that, my breathing starts to return to normal, but my heart is still racing. It has slowed a bit, but is still much faster than it should be.

"Do you want to go to the hospital? I'm worried; this is not normal."

"No, I don't I need to go to the hospital. I think I am having a panic attack; there is nothing the hospital can do for me."

"What's going on? We just had the best night in a very long time. Why would that make you have a panic attack? Come on, get dressed. I need to take you to the hospital," he says as he is trying to pull me out of the bed.

Staring back at him, it hits me. I feel as if I have

rewarded him for bad behavior. He did me wrong, and I am giving him a reward for it. What in the hell is wrong with me? How can I do this? It would be similar to me giving Blake or Isabella candy for feeding their dinner to the dog because they were tired of that particular meal.

I get out of the bed to head to the shower, angry with myself. "I'm fine. I will be fine. My heart will not allow me to reward you for bad behavior. I can't do this, not now, and I don't know how long before I can do it again." Before I turn back, I see his shoulders slumping, and shame crosses his face. I step out of the room into the bathroom, realizing the healing process is going to take longer than I had expected. I need more time before I can be intimate with him again. Even though it was awesome at the moment, my overanalyzing mind is having an internal fight with my heart. I step into the shower and let the warm water run over me, trying to soothe the panic.

When I step out of the bathroom, Grant is sitting at the edge of the bed, waiting for me; he's completely dressed. He motions to me with a pat on the mattress to go sit next to him. How do I go from fucking his brains out to wanting to beat them in? What the heck is wrong with me? I take a deep breath as I'm still trying to regulate my breathing while sitting next to him on the bed. He pulls me up and across his lap, hugging me. He hugs me so tight and close. "I am so sorry. I will tell you this every day because it's the truth. I will tell you how much I love you and need you everyday. But, please, don't leave me. I can't be without you. I will wait for you to be ready; this is all my fault."

I am shocked to hear him say that. Yes, he said it the day of the "cyber incident," but I must be living in my own head. I take control of everything, and I failed to see his need for me. He frames my face with his large hands and brings my eyes to his.

"I promise I'll give you all the time you need to get over what I've done to you. I hate myself for what I have done to you, to us. I wish I could take it back, but I can't. The only thing I can do is try to make it up to you. However long it takes for you to feel comfortable with being with me in this bed with you, in you, is how long I will wait for you. I have no interest in going back on any sites or having any chats with anyone other than you. Do you understand that, Shelby?"

It takes me a moment to respond to him, and he has really begun to heal my heart with his words. "Yes, but I don't know how long that will be."

"It doesn't matter how long. If it takes six months, I will be here. If it takes a year, I will be here. I did this to you. We haven't been apart since the day we met, and I will work for it. I will work for you to trust me again."

Wow, what a rollercoaster! I have no idea how long it will take me to get it together, but Grant's words on that bed in his arms really hit me. We are not the mushy couple that talks about feelings like that. But I felt his words as the truth. I know in my heart he is going to wait for me.

A couple of weeks pass with the same old same old— work, yoga, homework, cooking, and getting the kids to and from basketball and football practice. We have started to communicate even more. It's always nice to know that someone cares if you had a crappy day or a good day at work.

I have now dropped ten pounds and feel better in my own skin. Yoga has really helped tone my arms and belly. It gives me motivation to keep it going.

Grant and I have started a new bedtime routine without realizing it. When we get into bed, after the lights go out, we say our I Love Yous. I have been turning over away from him, but he did not let that stop him from showing me he loves me and will wait for me. Every night since my panic attack, when I turn away, he pulls me close to him, putting one arm under my neck and the other wrapped around my chest, with a hand on my heart. He whispers in my ear, "I will love you always and forever; please forgive me."

I thought it would get old, and he would eventually stop saying it. But he hasn't and I'm glad he didn't. It's helping me ward off the panic attacks; it has also helped me start to want him again and want to be with him again.

A few more weeks go by and just as he has told me every night for weeks, he says it again. But this time, I move my hand on top of his and say, "You are forgiven. I love you, Grant; I want to be close to you again. Our kids are getting older, and they don't occupy our time like they used to. They have their own friends, and I want to enjoy each other and our time together."

He holds me tighter, and with a shaky voice, asks, "Are you sure?" He will always feel bad for what he has done to me, and he should, but I have to move on.

I turn to face him, and I see the remorse in his eyes. "I

want to forget it and move on. Can you promise me you will never do anything like this again? Because I promise you, if you do, I will kill you!"

He chuckles. "I promise." With that, I feel such a sense of relief. Grant leans over to me, taking possession of my mouth as he moves his entire body over mine. We kiss each other so deep, with so much love. It reminds me of the first night Grant told me he loved me. We were making love to Air Supply on the radio; he looked me in the eyes as if he was looking into my soul and said, "I love you so much; I never want to be without you." We were engaged six months after meeting and married within a year. How time has flown by.

We spend the night making love like we did when we first met. We do things I never realized we had stopped doing—looking into each other's eyes as he moves in and out of me. It feels raw and real; our souls are wide open to each other. Grant keeps asking me if I am doing okay. I love that he is checking in with me, checking in on my mental health. I have become such a nutcase lately, and I am ready to move past that.

I wake the next morning feeling fantastic, feeling like our marriage has started over. When Grant senses I'm awake, he pulls me into his chest with his hand over my heart again. "I'm fine. You don't have to keep doing that."

I sense disappointment in his voice. "You don't like it when I hold you like this?"

"I love it when you do that, but I am getting better; you don't have to do that if you don't want to.

"I love to hold you like this. I can feel your heartbeat.

Your heartbeat is the truth to your soul, Shelby. I love holding it in my hand; it reminds me of how delicate you are under that tough-girl shell.

Chapter 8

Our sex life has taken off. We are now making love almost every night. Yes, that is what I said, almost every night! That's something I don't think we did on our honeymoon. The best part is we're doing it because we want to and not because we feel obligated. In the past, I thought, *Oh, hurry up, and get on with it; I am tired.* Now, we are up late making love because we both want to.

It's a boring Monday at work. Most of my co-workers are at a training secession I have already completed. I'm stuck manning the phones while everyone is out. However, all of our customers are at the same training, so it is dead around here. No emails and no phone calls. I'm bored out of my mind. I fire up my Kindle to read one of my smut books instead of sitting here doing nothing.

As I finish one particularly hot chapter, I look down at the lake from my window on the eleventh floor. It's a beautiful day outside this November morning. e had a hot summer, as usual, but it lasted longer than normal. The average temperatures were in the high eighties to the low nineties all the way through October. Today, it is finally cooling off; it's sixty-nine degrees with a nice breeze. The sun is beautifully dancing off the water of Lake Pontchartrain below. The sky is a bright blue with large white clouds.

On a day like today, I would love to work outside. I bet Grant loves today on the river. Not that he really wants to be at work or hanging over the Mississippi river in a harness, but I'm sure he is appreciating the cool weather. I know one thing Grant would really love is a sexy text from me. He would never expect it! We have been going strong but have yet to do anything different.

After the chapter I just finished, I have to admit, I am quite aroused and in need of a release. I am going to do something I would have never dreamed of doing prior to the "cyber incident," or prior to reading my newfound smut books. I hit the button on the phone to send all my calls to voicemail, and I head to the restroom with my iPhone.

I walk into the restroom and as I expected, it's empty. I go into the last stall, pull my tight hip-hugging pencil skirt up to my waist, and push my panties down to my knees. I am so turned on at the thought of what I'm about to do that I almost come without touching myself. I place my middle fingers gently between my lips, and they glide up and down easily in the wetness that has been waiting. Oh God, it feels so good, yet a voice in the back of my head asks me, "What in the hell are you doing?" I try my best to push that voice aside and proceed. With my left hand, I hit the camera app and lower the camera between my legs, taking a few snapshots of me masturbating.

While walking to the bathroom, I thought that I would just take a few snapshots to make it look as if I was doing myself, but I can't stop, not even to send the text. I continue to rub up and down my slick slit. I give myself more pressure with deep firm circles over my clit. If someone walks in right now, I am sure they will hear my labored breathing. But I hope they don't, because the only thing I can hear is my heart beating in my ears. My fingers start to move faster and deeper, that oh-so-familiar feeling is building, and I come with a tingle from head to toes. I got such a rush from doing this in the bathroom stall, yet I still can't believe I just did it. I try to regulate my breathing as I clean myself up then straighten my clothes. Once I am all put back together, I hear a voice again. But this is a voice I've never heard before. I have heard women talk about their inner sex goddess, but I have never had that voice. I've only heard the one telling me what not to do—the one that tells me what's inappropriate. But I hear a different voice now, and she asks me, "Why haven't you ever done this before? Please plan on doing it again; it was amazing."

I pull my text messages up and hit Grant's name.

Shelby 2:50 p.m.
Thinking of you
r u busy?

Grant 2:51
Not too busy watching my guys work
mk sure they don't set any fires
What u thinking?

Shelby 2:52
U better hold onto your phone bc I am about to set your phone on fire
I was thinking of you
& had to run to the restroom
Want to see what I hv been up to?

I choose the best out of the six photos I snapped and send him two pictures. The first picture shows my fingers over my slit. It's very sexy; my perfectly painted red nails looks picture perfect. In the second picture there are no fingernails to be seen. They have slipped into my pussy, and you can actually see my wetness dripping down to my ass. OMG, I sure hope he has all his safety equipment on when he opens this text, or he may be swimming in the Mississippi River today.

Grant 2:55
OMG that is the sexiest thing I have ever seen
Did u make yourself come?

Shelby 2:56
Why else would I bother?

Grant 2:56
I am going to be stuck in this harness w/a hard on until knock off time w/that in mind

Shelby 2:57
Keep it that way
Meet me in the bathroom when u get home
we can get a few min in b4 the kids game!
U in?

Grant 2:59
Am I in? what kind of ques is that?

As long as I don't fall off this scaffold and drown I will be there waiting for you after my shower.

Chapter 9

"Grant"

My brain is still frozen on the images in the text I just received from Shelby. I almost dropped my phone into the freaking river when I saw them. To see those sexy red fingernails about to enter her pussy! Her fingers pressed deep inside of her with excitement dripping down the crack of her ass. I will be stuck in the harness hanging over the river all day with a hard on. That was so hot, so fucking sexy! Where in the hell did this come from?

The guilt sets in. Why didn't I suggest this to her before I broke her down and destroyed her trust? Damn it! I have to treat her better. I have to show her how much I love her and appreciate the changes she has made. I am going to stop at the flower shop on the way home from work to pick her up something.

As I sit here and watch my welders weld on this beautiful day, my mind drifts to how thankful I am that she didn't kick me out for what I've done to her. I know I rationalized it in my head as an extension of porn. I told myself it was not cheating on her, but it was. Even though I never touched another woman, I was cheating on Shelby's heart. I knew she was a strong woman, but I had no idea she would be able to handle the situation as she has.

She has had many ups and downs in the last two months. I told her I would wait as long as it takes for her to be ready, and that is the truth. I would have waited a lifetime if she needed it. She's my life; she keeps everything going, our kids, our house, our finances, and our love. She's the key to everything that is us.

We've had some really intense sex in the last few weeks. It has been almost every day of the week. I didn't want to push her to do anything out of her comfort zone. But, man, seeing this text, I have to believe her comfort zone is growing. But I will let it grow at it's own pace. I can't push her, I won't!

"Shelby"

When I get home from work, Isabella is upstairs getting ready for her basketball game, and Blake is playing video games. They come down to kiss me and tell me hello. They are excited to bring me to the kitchen table to show me the flowers their father brought home for me. When I walk into the kitchen, I see a beautiful bouquet of fall flowers in deep reds and oranges sitting on the table. I tell them to finish up what they were doing while I go get changed; we have to leave in twenty minutes.

I open the bathroom door just as Grant steps out of the shower with a wide smile on his face. I lock the door behind me. He drops his towel and steps toward me, "Hey, my dirty girl! Do you know how much it turned me on to get those pictures from you today?" One of his arms wraps around my waist, already pulling me close, as his other hand goes into the back of my hair bringing my face to his.

"I could only imagine how much that turned you on, but why don't you show me instead?"

Looking down at his penis, he says, "This is what I have been sporting all day!" I look down to see him half-erect. Not limp, but not fully at attention.

Looking up into his eyes with determination, I say, "We have about eighteen minutes before we have to leave for Isabella's game, that is not going to cure the need in my pussy right now!"

Grant's beautiful green eyes get big; he's shocked by my words. "Well, what are you going to do to fix that?" I pull my vanity chair over to me and sit facing him. He is standing in front of me naked. I grab him around his hips, pull him toward me, and lick his dick from the tip to the base. I am rewarded with a moan of approval. With a few long strides of my tongue, he is now at full attention. I put my hands on his ass to guide his cock in and out of my mouth, pushing him as deep as I can go then pulling him back out. The next time in, I open my lips a little wider and take more of him in. Once I have taken him in a few times with my tongue sliding back and forth on the underside of his cock, I am as deep as I can go. I remove one of my hands from his ass to massage his balls. He is so hard right now, and the throbbing in between my legs is getting more intense. He pulls out before I can protest, lifts me out of the chair, pulls my skirt up around my waist, and rips my panties off by the side seam.

Seeing I was not happy about the tearing of my panties, he promises to buy me a few new pairs as an anniversary gift. He lifts me by my ass and sits me on the bathroom counter, right on the edge. He pushes my heels up on the edge and thrusts inside of me. His roughness makes me gasp, but it feels amazing. At this angle, spread-eagle with my knees up, it's so deep. My back is against the mirror, and my palms are on the countertop while Grant pushes in and out of me with force. I start to moan as quietly as I can; we don't want to attract the kid's attention.

I am very close to going over the edge as Grant says, "Show me how you touched yourself today. Please, Shelby, I want to see how you fucked yourself today." I follow his instructions and raise my hand from the counter, sliding my hand past my hips, putting my finger on my clit, and rubbing in circles, while I watch his cock go in and out of me. It's such a turn on that my desire takes over and sends my body into the ultimate pleasure. When my orgasm winds down, Grant picks up the pace. He comes, sending me into a second orgasm. The feeling is so different from the first—it's exposed and heated.

I look up at the clock to see we now have less than five minutes to get dressed and leave. Grant pulls me forward to meet his firm chest and kisses me. His kiss is very gentle as he looks into my eyes. "Thank you. Thank you for coming back to me, for letting me love you again. We are going to make it! I promise you, I will make an effort every day to make sure you know I love you and that you can trust me."

We get ourselves together and make it to the gym just in time. Grant and I sit close to each other; we feel like we need to be connected to each other at all times now.

Chapter 10

As we watch Isabella play her game, I realize our anniversary is coming soon! Grant mentioned it earlier, but I had totally forgotten with everything going on. What am I going to get him? What would he want? Maybe his all-time number-one fantasy? I don't know, he may have to settle for his number-two fantasy, but I am not even sure I can do that.

The buzzer at the end of the game brings me out of my daydream. Isabella's team has won which means to the team and the parents we are going out for pizza. It's always a good time with this group of parents. She has been on this team for six years, and we know them all well.

We enter the restaurant, and everyone knows the drill. The kids sit at one table and the parents at the other. The men have settled at the end of the table near the large TV screens on the wall to watch a football game. The ladies have started to order margaritas.

I have become particularly close to two of the mothers, Karen and Samantha. They corner me at the table and ask me what the heck is going on with Grant and me. I am shocked and embarrassed that they noticed. Karen looks up over her frozen drink. "Girl, spill it. We know something is up. For the last two months, you looked like you hated his guts, and now, you two can't keep your hands off one another."

I take a long sip of my margarita before spilling it all.

As the words are coming out of my mouth, I can't believe I am saying them out loud. Once it is all out on the table, I can see they are a little shocked. Grant and I are the all-American couple; we have it all, or so it looked that way from the outside—married young, two kids, a boy and a girl, a beautiful house, nice cars, great jobs, and after almost twenty years, we still appeared happily married. I mean, really, that is a big deal; there aren't many in today's society that are married that long. Everyone else is on their second or third marriage.

The girls order our second round of drinks, and Samantha puts her hand on mine and gives it a squeeze. " Everything is going to be fine. Be glad it happened this way. At least you were able to put a stop to it." She tells us how her first husband started chatting online, and he met up with what he thought was a woman. The joke was on him—it was a guy! She caught them in bed right as he found out his date was a gay guy! "It was too late for me, because at that point, the damage was done. It was not his love for me that stopped him from screwing her … I mean him. Whatever, the only reason he did not sleep with his date was because she had a dick."

"So you're saying I am lucky since I caught it before it went there? I have to admit this situation has made me re-evaluate myself, girls. I have found a voice in my head that I have never heard before. Have ya'll ever heard people talk about their inner sex goddess?"
Karen's eyes get big and she bounces up and down in her chair, with her hand in the air, and yells, "Oh yea, me, me! I have one of those. I won't even tell ya'll what she makes me do. I love to hear her voice."

We all laugh with her. I tell them about my anniversary coming up on Monday. I ask for help on what to get Grant. This is a big one, twenty years, and I have put zero thought into getting something for him. That's so unlike me; by nature, I go overboard with plans, but I have been derailed by the past events and need their help. After another round of margaritas. we decide it has to be sex related. I tell them I know of a little store that is near my office, one of those kinky stores. But I wouldn't know the first thing about what to buy from there. Karen is very excited about meeting me there and helping me out.

"I think this is something I have to do on my own, Karen. I appreciate the offer, but I think I will fly solo on this one."

She gives me a silly frown, "You can go by yourself, but tell us what Grant's top three fantasies are, so we can suggest what to buy. I am sure they are the same as every other guy, but I just want to make sure."

This chick must be out of her freaking mind. I'm a very private person, and the only reason I have spilled this much information is due to the amount of alcohol I have consumed and the stress of keeping it to myself. But the drinks keep coming. Every now and then, the guys turn, looking to see what's so funny. We are getting a bit loud as we laugh hysterically at just about everything. Now on our third margarita, they ask again about Grant's fantasies. Yep, you guessed it, it just flies right out of my mouth. I tell them with red cheeks that number one is me with another woman. I keep my eyes down, looking at my drink. I look up when Samantha loses it. She is laughing hard and slapping her hand on the table trying to regain her composure. She is almost falling out of her chair with laughter.

"Samantha, get it together. What's your problem?" I ask as I slap her hand. "I never said I would do it! You asked a question, and I answered it."

She finally catches her breath, "Don't you know that's every man's number one? What rock have you lived under, my friend?"

Karen elbows her hard to stop her from carrying on so much and gives me a gentle smile with a confirming nod to let me know Samantha is correct. She then puts her hand over mine, "Can I take a wild guess at number two? Let me guess, is it anal sex?"

"Holy fucking shit! Have I really been living under a rock? I guess you all know number three is in public, right?" Samantha smiles and nods her head yes in confirmation.

"You do know it has to be daylight outside, right?" Of course, I did not know that! I look at them with fear in my eyes. "What in the hell am I supposed to do about this?"

Samantha looks at me seriously. "If you ever decide you want to do number one, I know a woman who does that."

"What? Are you nuts? You know a hooker that you want me to sleep with?" I am thinking I shouldn't have started this conversation with these two. Actually, I shouldn't have started this conversation with Samantha. I knew she was always a little looser than the rest of us, but I chalked it up to her being younger. Now, she is looking at me with her lips pressed tightly together in a straight line and her arms crossed as if I have offended her, because I think she just suggested I give my husband a freaking hooker for his anniversary.

"No, no, no, Shelby, she's not a hooker. Hookers sleep with men who can't get it elsewhere. This woman is a marriage counselor." She uses her fingers to put quotes around marriage counselor. "She is a sex therapist. which is legal, anything you do or say to her is confidential. It's not for everyone; she will determine if that particular scene is what the two of you need. But get this, Shelby, it's covered by your insurance. Everything is protected by the patient privacy act; no one knows what you're doing in there. While her practice may not be conventional, it works well in certain cases."

Karen and I sit and stare at her; we are speechless. I slowly look over to Karen to see if she's still breathing. She's just shaking her head back and forth before she says a word. "Samantha, you are crazy to believe that something like that exists! Do you actually know someone who claims to have seen this doctor?" For the first time in six years, I see Samantha blush. "Oh no, you didn't, did you?"

She still looks flushed as she leans into Karen. "Oh yes, I did, and it was one of the best sexual experiences I have ever had. I can't say I would do it again, but I don't regret it."

"Why would you do that? What would make you want to do that? You have never had issues with Phillip like Grant and I, right?"

We are now whispering to each other in a tight circle. "After the Internet thing with my first husband, I vowed I would never ignore my new husband's fantasies. Every now and then, we get a little freaky and try something different. That was one of those times."

The men have walked over to our end of the table. Grant comes up behind my chair and puts his hands on my shoulders, massaging them as he stands there. Poor Phillip. He has no idea what he is in for when he opens his mouth and asks, "What ya'll talking about over here? It sounds like a lot of fun."

Samantha pipes up, "Just gossiping about you sexy hunks, you know, comparing shoes sizes." That throws them off. They don't have a response, nor do they want to touch Samantha's comment with a ten-foot pole. We further distract them by asking them to go get us to-go cups for the margaritas we have not finished. This is one thing I miss when I visit other places—my to-go cup. I love living in the New Orleans area! We all say our goodbyes. Grant drives us home as he is the designated driver.

Chapter 11

The weekend flies by with laundry, grocery shopping, and cooking for the week taking up most of my daytime hours. Grant and I had another wonderful weekend of lovemaking once the lights were out. But today is Monday, and it's our anniversary. I woke to a beautifully wrapped gift box sitting on Grant's empty pillow. I sit up to unwrap my gift, finding three very skimpy thongs. I can't stop smiling as I remember his promise to buy me new panties the day he ripped mine off in the bathroom. I open the card.

"To the love of my life. Thanks for the best twenty years of my life, looking forward to many more."

I'm now at my desk, but I can't stop thinking about what Samantha said Friday night. Was she drunk? Could she have been really telling the truth? Almost as if she has ESP, my cell beeps with a text from her.

Samantha 9:50 a.m.
Shared Contact - Dr. Love
Just in case you need this
If you have the guts girl u wont regret it

Shelby 9:55 a.m.
Thanks for the info
Not sure this is for us

Samantha 9:56 a.m.
If u want to talk abt it let me know
If not I will never say another word
Code word u will need IF you call
"Devastated"

Shelby 9:57
Thanks

That girl is nuts. The reality is this is too much, too
soon for me. I'm thinking we start backward with number
three. I can handle outside in the hot tub after the kids go
to sleep; I can do that. Shit, they said it had to be daylight.
I will have to do this my way. Baby steps.

Today is our twentieth wedding anniversary, and I
have put off getting Grant something, so I have to do it
today. I will take my lunch hour to hit the lingerie/sex
toyshop. I get back to work answering e-mails and daily
reports. Noon arrives before I have time to talk myself out
of my trip to Mandy's Romantic Boutique. I drive over
with a nervous stomach; I have never been inside a place
like this before so I don't know what to expect. I pull into
the parking lot to see that I'm the only car there. Damn it, I
will have the salesperson's full attention. I hate an
overbearing salesperson, just leave me alone so I can be on
my way.

The bell above the door rings as I walk in. There are
two women standing at the counter to greet me. One is an
elderly lady in her mid-seventies with heavy makeup, and
she is dressed conservatively in a suit. The other is a young

woman in her early twenties with lots of cleavage pushed up over her corset top, a very short skirt, fishnet stockings, and army boots. Her hair is dyed turquoise blue with almost everything on her face pierced, and most exposed skin is tattooed. The younger woman walks around the counter and asks if she can help me find anything specific. As I mentally will my face not blush, I tell her I am looking for a blindfold and silk restraint set.

The young girl smiles widely and pushes past the elderly lady. "Oh fun. I love that stuff; follow me to the fun section." Walking behind her, I take in the items of the store. Sexy nighties, corsets, stockings, masquerade-style masks, and club wear. Meanwhile, she introduces herself as Candy. Candy pushes back a curtain, and we enter another room sectioned off from the rest of the store. She lets it close behind us, and we are in a twelve-foot-by-twelve-foot room filled with sex toys.

Again, I'm trying not to blush, trying to maintain my composure as she gives me the rundown of what's on the wall. "This is the restraint section; there is a wide variety of items here. For starters, we have this simple set of hand restraints and a blindfold. For more advanced sets, this one has four full restraints for each limb and a ball gag." Yes, this is what she is telling me; nobody can make this shit up. "So, ya'll are beginners, right? Do you need the ball gag?"

"The beginner set is exactly what I was looking for, thank you."

"Oh, I got ya, beginners. You may want to buy a whip or a crop if restraints are being used. This will enhance the experience, I promise."

I am not even sure how to respond to this girl, as she stands there nonchalantly popping bubbles with her gum.

"Thanks, Candy, but I think the beginner restraint set will work well for now. I work right up the street. I can pass by another day if I need any additional items. But thanks for the suggestion."

She proceeds to ask me some very personal questions. I am not sure why I'm even answering her, but I do.

"Look, don't be embarrassed; this is my job. I see all kinds of people come in and out of that door. I like to help. It's my job to know all of these products in order to help my customers. And let me tell ya, I KNOW all of these products, very well. How long have you been married?"

"Today is our twentieth anniversary; I'm just looking to try something a little different."

"Oh, I see you read that book too? I figured this kind of stuff is not the norm for you, so let me help. I want you to be the sex goddess I know you can be."

Yea, the blushing is out the window now; this is just weird at this point. Candy does not miss a beat.

"Sorry, I don't mean to offend you; sex talk is a part of my everyday work life. If I am being too intrusive, just tell me to shut the fuck up," she says with a grin.

I decide to just go with it because she really does seem sincere. "No, Candy, you are fine. I obviously need help, so why not take it from the woman at the sex store who is willing to give it to me for free? My mother taught me never to kick a gift horse in the mouth; what do you suggest?"

"Do you have a picture of your husband on your

phone?" I thought it would be rude to refuse, so I show her a picture of us. "Wow, you two are a beautiful couple; what a sexy man you have there. What a perfect match you two are. Hey, a friend of mine is having a New Year's Eve party in the French Quarter—it's a private event. Actually, it's a very exclusive party, by invitation only. I have five invitations to give out and only two of them left. He instructed me to only give them to attractive couples." She grabs my arm lightly with a concerned look on her face. I assume she can tell I'm about to dart out of the room. "Please don't freak out. I'm not coming on to you, and this is not a swingers only club, but if you are willing to share, it's welcomed there."

I don't respond to her immediately; my mouth can't form words. I think I'm in a state of shock!

"It's like any other club, but sexier. Everyone is dressed for sex, if you know what I mean?" No, I have no idea what she means; the look on my face can tell her that.

"You will love it. The first floor is a ballroom set up with a bar and a dance floor. Once you have had a few drinks, you make your way up to the second floor. But only if you're okay with seeing people having sex everywhere! It's crazy, in a good way. You don't have to participate; you can just watch. As a married couple of twenty years, it will be fun for ya'll to observe. Or, you can find a bed, and do each other right there in front of everyone."

I start to laugh nervously, and she notices she is making me a bit uncomfortable.

"I'm sorry. I shouldn't have assumed you would be comfortable with that stuff. Please do me a favor; please don't make up your mind right now. I'm really good at picking out who will do well at these parties, and I know if you give it some thought, you and your husband will go and have a wild time."

Do I have "talk sex with me" written on my freaking forehead, and I don't know it? What is the deal? Samantha tells me about her girl-on-girl doctor visit, and now, a total stranger at the sex store invites Grant and me to an exclusive sex party at a club in the French Quarter. And of all things, my stupid sex goddess is poking her little head out, jumping up and down, clapping her hands, and yelling at me, "Come on, Shelby, that sounds like fun; tell her we will go. She said you don't have to be a swinger. Sex is everywhere; please, please, please, say yes, pretty please!" I mean, really, are you fucking kidding me? I am hearing this in my own head.

I am lost in my head listening to my sex goddess when I hear Candy say, "I will leave you alone to make your final selection. I will also get that invitation for you."

"Thanks, Candy, I appreciate it, and I'm sorry for being freaked out, but you are right; this is not the norm for me."

"It's okay. I'm used to it; it's my job to push you to be the best sex goddess you can be."

With that, she leaves me alone in the room. OMG, there is some crazy shit in here. Never mind the stuff, I think I just agreed to take an invitation to a sex party. Yet, standing there looking at all of the items and thinking of the party is making me wet. I feel as if I have discovered something inside of myself that I never knew was there.

Do I really want to know this new me? *Shelby, focus on the task at hand*, I tell myself as my mind is running wild. I see the simple gift set I want; the package contains a black eye mask and two royal purple silk ties. Purple is my favorite color. Grant is going to be so surprised when he opens this as an anniversary gift. I decide this is enough for today. I have already purchased some sexy lingerie online, not to mention, at some point, I will have to tell Grant about the sex party. If I decide I have enough nerve to attend.

Candy rings me up at the register, and I head to the door with my purchase. She runs out from around the counter to give me a big hug which is not surprising; we are pretty touchy-feely here in the south. We hug everyone after meeting them as a greeting. She takes this opportunity to whisper in my ear, "The invitation and application are in your bag." I give her a perplexed look as she walks me to the door away from the elderly lady watching us. "Shelby, not just anybody can show up at this type of event. This is a big deal to be invited if you're not a member. You have paperwork to look over and sign. You know, confidential stuff promising you wont share what you see there. They will also need your identification information to make sure you're not a criminal. You will get an access card in the mail a few days before the party. They will also have a form you and your husband need to get completed by their doctor if you plan on swapping anything with anyone. Now, get out of here, girl, and have a good time tonight with that hunk of a man you have."

Once I get to my car, I'm a bit overwhelmed. My

hands are shaking so much I have a hard time getting the keys into the ignition. Am I really going to tell Grant about this party? I feel the continued throbbing between my legs and take that as a sigh that says yes. I can't focus on that; I have to focus on our anniversary first. I head to the local drugstore for giftwrap. I wrap the gift in my car, and I pull out the invitation Candy put in the bag. The invitation is very elaborate. On thick lavender stock paper, there is beautiful writing in raised silver lettering:

You have been invited to the most
Exclusive Party of the Year.
We want to ring in the New Year with YOU!
9:00 P.M.
Savannah's Closet
Corner of St. Ann & Bourbon Street

Details to follow after verification process has been completed. See the
required info attached. Looking forward to seeing you there!

I sit there and stare at it. Am I really interested in doing this? I'm not sure this is something I'm interested in, even though I just told myself two seconds ago that I was. I need time to think about it, but I only have a month to decide. We are now in mid-October, and evaluations have to be completed by the end of November. I shake my head and put the paperwork in my bag for later. When I finally get back to my desk, the phone is ringing with a call from the front desk. "Hey, Shelby, it's Sue; there is a customer up front to see you. Can you come up here please?"

"Sure, Sue, I'll be right up." I wonder who that could

be; I don't have any scheduled appointments today.

I walk up to the front entrance to find a lady standing there with a very large arrangement of red roses. "Hi, are you Ms. Chauvin?" I nod my head in confirmation. "There is no way you can carry this massive arrangement back to your desk, but I can roll them back there if you like."

"Thanks, I would really appreciate that. Follow me; I'll show you the way."

"I have never delivered twenty roses before—such an odd number—is it a special number for you?"

"Actually, it's my twentieth wedding anniversary." We are finally at my desk, and Ms. Nosey Rosie checks out all the pictures on my desk as she waits for me to lift the heavy vase onto my desk. Her eyes find a picture of Grant and me.

"No way. Twenty years? Ya'll barely look thirty-five, how can you be married twenty years?" With a sigh, I tip her for the compliment as I did the heavy lifting. I smile politely at her. "We married young, and I am much older than you suspect." Taking her tip, she smiles back and is on her way.

I pick up the phone and dial Grant to thank him for the flowers and the panties from this morning. I snap a photo of them and text him a picture.

"Hey, Bossy Girl," he answers.

"Thank you so much for the beautiful flowers; they are exquisite. I am the envy of the office. And thanks for replacing my unmentionables that you damaged the other day." I smile and hear him chuckle on the other end.

"I am glad you like the flowers, but nothing is as beautiful as you are. I love you so much. Happy Anniversary."

"That melts my heart. I love you too, and Happy Anniversary, babe."

"And those panties—don't get too attached to them; I plan on ripping them off every chance I get. If I have to buy a pair every payday just to rip them off, I will do that. I plan on giving you everything you need for the next twenty years. I love you, Shelby."

"I love you too. I have to go, but do me a favor and check the bathroom closet when you get home. That's where I left your gift." Before he has a chance to ask any questions, I hang up with a sly smile.

Chapter 12

I hope to get home before Grant does so I have time to hide his gift in the bathroom closet. I don't want to have to explain to the kids what I bought for Dad! Thankfully, I make it home thirty minutes before he does. When Grant walks in from work, I am standing at the stove cooking. The kids are at the table doing homework. It looks like any other day of the week. He puts his arms around my waist and kisses me gently on my neck. Oh, how I love when he kisses the back of my neck like that; it always sends shivers down my spine.

I feel something cold run down my neck and in between my breasts. When I look down, I see a silver-and-diamond heart necklace.

He whispers in my ear, "Happy Anniversary, babe."

I turn into his arms so quickly to kiss him, I forget I'm still holding the spoon I was using to stir the red beans with. The necklace is so beautiful, I don't even care that I have just swung red beans across half the kitchen. I'll clean that later. "Oh, Grant, you didn't have to buy me this. But it's stunning. I love it, and thank you."

"I know I didn't have to, I wanted to. Look, it has exactly twenty diamonds in it. I had it specially made for this anniversary."

"I don't know what to say; my gift is not nearly this nice."

"I am sure I will love whatever you bought as long as it came from you. I love you so much. Let me go take a shower before dinner. Is that okay? Do I have time?"

"Yes, but don't take all day; the kids are starving." He heads off to the bathroom as the kids start asking homework questions. A few minutes later, I hear my phone beep with a text. It's Grant. He's texting me from the bathroom.

Grant 4:45 p.m.
This is one of the best gifts you have ever bought me
To a man this is Diamonds
I can't wait 2 tie you up 2night
The things I will make u feel tonight will blow your mind

Shelby 4:46
glad u like it
I can't wait
Is it time to for the kids to go to bed yet?

Grant 4:46
I wish!

We sit through dinner acting like teenagers. We smirk and giggle at each other with lots of touching under the table. The kids pick up that we are acting weird. Isabella demands to know what we are giggling about. Blake pipes up, "Never mind them, Isabella, it's their anniversary, and they are just being gross and mushy!" After dinner, the kids and Grant clean the kitchen and dishes while I take a shower. I take my time exfoliating, shaving all necessary areas, and moisturizing.

I move my new sexy outfit and high heels to the bathroom closet for easy access later. Grant has not seen this part of his surprise. Walking out of the bathroom, I literally run into Grant's hard chest as he is coming into the room. He boxes me in with his arms and leans over me. With a slow sultry voice, he says, "I can't wait to fuck you until you can't walk straight tomorrow."

"Is that a promise, handsome? You know, I don't like broken promises." I escape under his arm and look back at him over my shoulder and blow him a kiss. I head to the fridge to pour wine for the two of us. We sit on the sofa together, watch the news, and catch up on the day's activities. The kids are in and out of the room getting ready for bed and packing school bags for tomorrow. Finally, it's their bedtime. We all say our goodnights, and they head upstairs.

We head off to our room, and I rush ahead of Grant, locking the bathroom door behind me. I reach for my secret stash of sexy wear, pulling out my corset. It's beautiful; the fabric is a silky garnet red embellished with roses and it has a matching G-string. I had already tried it on and fitted the strings as these things are not easy to put on alone. The first time, it took me over twenty minutes just to get the strings right. But now that the back has been tied, it's as easy as buttoning up the front and putting on the panties.

But you can't wear a corset without thigh-highs. I went a little over the top and bought black fishnet thigh-highs. They look very sexy with my platform heels, which have not been worn in over five years. They are so high they have a two-hour limit on them. Considering I plan on being on my back most of the time, they should do the job. That's if I can make it out of the bathroom without falling flat on my face.

Right before I try my stripper walk out of the bathroom, I sweep my hair up in a messy twist in the back with strands of hair falling on each side of my face. I put on a little foundation, just enough to not look like I have make up on, but enough to look fresh faced. For the final touch, I put on ruby red smudge-proof lipstick.

I'm surprised when I open the door leading to the bedroom; it's fully lit with candles. Grant is sitting on the edge of the bed with the blindfold and ties in his hand. He looks up and down my body as he holds his hand out for me to come stand in front of him.

I walk over to him, but he stops me an arm's distance away. "I want to take a minute to take you in, Shelby. That is so sexy; you look hot." He places his hands on my hips and rubs them up the sides of my corset, feeling my curves under the satin fabric. As his hands reach the top, he lightly runs his fingers over my now rounded breasts that have been pushed up by the tight corset. I shiver from the pleading look in his eyes combined with his touch.

"Turn around for me? Let me see you from behind. Oh, you are so beautiful. Do you know how much I love your ass? And that thong is getting me so hard." His hands are roaming all over my ass and thighs. I am getting wet quickly, and my heart races when Grant slips a silk tie onto one of my wrists. Turning me around, he kisses me urgent and needy, keeping his eyes open..

He slips the blindfold over my eyes, kisses my lips, and lays me down on our king-sized bed. My senses are heightened with my eyes covered. He has laid me down diagonally across the bed, and I feel my feet hit the pillows at the top. My hands are pulled above my head with my free hand wrapped in the tie. I open my hands to wrap them around the post of our large four-post bed. More silk ties are wrapped around my ankle. Where in the heck did he get more silk ties? What is he doing? "Grant, what are you doing?" I say, as he rubs his hand across my belly, sending involuntary shivers up my spine.

"Shh, Shelby, I am in control; I know how much of a control freak you are, so I am going to have to tie your feet also."

"Where did you get the other ties? You didn't know I bought this gift until today, right?"

"No, babe, I had no idea you bought this, but it took you a few minutes to get ready which gave me some time to think. I thought about how you needed to be tied down completely. I went through the closet and found three silk robes and knew that's what I needed."

While he's talking, I feel his hands gently around my ankles as my foot is being tied to the post. I ask him, "Three, why do you need three?" He doesn't answer, but I figure it out; my left leg is close to the headboard, but there is no way my right leg would reach the other post with one wrap. I hear him tie the two together so my legs are stretched wide apart, but not uncomfortably. It is amazing how much you can hear simply because your eyes are covered.

Once I'm completely tied, I feel and hear nothing! I give it a second before I start to panic, then I feel Grant's breath on my face. It is so sensual to have the blindfold on. Every inch of my body is on high alert. With no thought to it, I reach my tongue out and connect with his mouth instantly. I have absolutely no control—no control over the position of my head, the depth of his tongue, nothing! But it feels exquisite and different.

After kissing me deeply, he roams my body with his hands, running them over the top of my breasts, down my bodice, and over my fishnet stockings. His hands come up again to the top of my corset, and I feel the first few buttons being undone just enough to allow my cleavage to be freed. Between each movement, he pauses, giving me time to anticipate his next move. Although I cannot see anything, I can almost feel what he'll do next.

The bed dips, and I feel his warm breath on my nipple. He circles my nipple with his tongue, slowly and gently at first. I arch my back to push my breast closer to him. He nips at me with his teeth, and I let out a breathy moan. A pinch of pain from his teeth is followed by a sensation of ecstasy. My nipples are hard and erect as he pulls away from me.

The other side of the bed dips, and he does the same to the other nipple while keeping the abandoned one erect by rolling it between his fingers. Then he's gone. I listen closely trying to hear what he's doing, but he has turned his iPhone on and is playing music. With the background noise, it's difficult to anticipate what he's doing. However, I do hear a drawer shut! Grant is now straddling me with his knees on the sides of my hips.

Leaning over near my ear, he whispers, "Let me know if there is something you don't like, or if I'm hurting you. I want to test your limits. Do you trust me to test your limits, Shelby?"

I nod my head yes quickly.

"Just say STOP if it's too much for you; promise me you will stop me if it's too intense for you."

"I will, I promise." Before my brain can even begin to imagine what I'll have to tell him stop for, I feel a tight pinch on my right nipple! It hurts for a second, but just as his teeth did earlier, ecstasy follows. I feel what might be a chain across my chest, it's cold but light. The left nipple gets the same pinch. Grant pulls on what I believe is a chain attaching whatever is clamped onto my nipples. Oh Lord, the biting pain creates such a pulling pleasure. "I am about to come that is sending electricity straight to my pussy."

"Breathe through it. You can do it. If you wait to come, it will be beyond anything you've ever experienced." With slow breaths, I am able to push away the sensation of my release. I'm not sure I'll be able to do this much longer— the feeling is too amazing. Lost in my concentration of not coming, I notice he's gone again. He really has to stop this disappearing act.

I can sense him standing next to the bed on my right. I turn my head in that direction, feeling the heated skin of his hard cock on my lips. I open my mouth to allow him to push in. I have very little ability to move my head and gladly take what he's giving me. I suck him as deep as I can. I run my tongue on the bottom of him as he pulls out. He's moaning loudly, and it's such a turn-on to feel this powerful and in control, even with all my limbs bound.

I can tell by his labored breathing he's close to coming, and he pulls away from me. Quickly moving around the bed, he's now in between my legs. I feel my panties being moved to the side slowly.

"This thong is way too sexy to rip."

Then I feel nothing. I plead with him, "I am about to burst; please let me come." I can almost see the smile on his face right now, as he knows how impatient I am.

"I am just admiring the view; if you only knew how fucking hot you look tied to the bed like this. But I aim to please. Are you saying you want me to touch your pussy, Shelby?"

"Oh yes, Grant, I'm having a hard time up here trying to contain myself … please," I plead again.

"Or do you want me to lick it?"

I reply in a very out of breath voice, "I don't give a shit what you do, just do something." He chuckles and licks me slowly from the crack of my ass to the top of my engorged clit.

The feeling is multiplied by being tied and blindfolded. He continues to stroke his tongue up and down my slit, and slowly, I arch my hips to get more pressure, but he pushes me down. "Don't be in such a rush; enjoy it." I feel his finger enter me. He starts to pump his finger in and out at the same slow rhythm his tongue is moving over my clit.

I feel a second finger added, and it feels wonderfully full. His fingers move in and out a little faster, and his tongue makes circles over my clit, adding more pressure. My breathing is louder in my ears, and my moans are uncontrolled. Grant reaches up, pulling on the chain that's attached to my nipples, and the pressure building within me explodes. My orgasm rocks my entire body, and I feel a wave of pleasure washing over my entire body.

Not being able to touch him is torture. I want to reach out and grab him, wrap my arms around him, and feel his naked chest on mine. I want to hear his heart beat. As these thoughts run through my mind, Grant leans over me with his knees on each side of my hips and embraces me. His big hands go under my back as he pulls me up to his chest while kissing my neck in that sweet spot right under my ear. The chills break out all over my body again! I need him right now; I need to feel him inside of me.

"I need you inside of me now. Please fuck me as hard as you can; I need it, you need it, and we need it. Please, Grant," I beg.

"This is so erotic. I love this anniversary gift. Thank you, Shelby, this is the best gift ever. Now, I am going to untie your feet and flip you with your hands still tied to the post, putting you on your elbows and knees. Then I'm going to fuck you so hard, you will beg me to stop. Do you trust me not to hurt you, Shelby?"

"Yes, I trust you; please fuck me!" And he does just that. Putting both of his strong arms under me, he turns me over onto my belly. I raise myself up onto my elbows and knees with my hands held tightly onto the bedpost for support.

I feel him behind me. "You are so beautiful; you have

the most beautiful pussy. I love the way you taste. I know I said I was going to fuck you, but I can't resist licking you just one more time.

"Oh God, please, I need you inside of me." I am begging now. My ass is high in the air, and my face is down on the mattress with my chest resting on my forearms. After a few sultry licks, I feel Grant's body close to my ass, his dick at my entrance as he rubs it up and down in my wetness. His hard cock slides in just a little, only giving me a little at a time to make it last. He knows I am ready to come again. He likes to tease me. He feels so thick. I can tell by his breathing that he is enjoying this even more than I am. I haven't been able to touch him or see him, but I can tell he is very close to coming also.

While his cock continues to go deeper, I feel something wet dripping down the crack of my ass. I'm a bit startled by it, but I'm in such a catatonic state it almost feels too far away to notice. Grant rocks in and out of me at a pace that is slow and deep. If I had any more room on these restraints, I would push back on him to give him more of me and push him deeper, if that's even possible.

Grant's hands are rubbing over the roundness of my ass. They feel very slippery, with oil possibly, and then I feel his finger gently rubbing down the crack of my ass. It makes me a bit nervous, but the rhythmic rocking has me in a trance. His finger slowly circles my forbidden hole. It's shameful and sexy all at the same time. The feeling of his finger making circles around my hole in the same rhythm as his cock going in and out of my pussy is unbelievable. It feels better than I could have ever imagined.

I think his finger may have slipped in slightly, but the

only thing I can feel is pleasure. I can't distinguish the difference between his cock in my pussy or his finger in my ass. All I know is it feels so fucking good that I don't want it to stop. He leans over me to whisper in my ear, "Does that feel good? Do you like this?"

I respond with a moan. "Everything you are doing feels like heaven. Please don't stop." And he doesn't. I feel so full; it's an odd feeling, yet so satisfying and forbidden.

He takes his time with my ass and my pussy. He has definitely pushed the bar on our sexual experiences. My thoughts swirl around in my head. *Is this Pandora's box? What will this open up for us?* There are so many erotic things I have never allowed my mind to consider. This is one thing I would have never considered, yet it feels so good. We have to try more. I have to allow Grant to push me. I want to end every weekend by saying that was the most erotic thing I have ever experienced!

Grant's rocking has increased, and I feel my orgasm building, but it feels very different with the added pressure. When my orgasm hits me, it's mind blowing. My body goes rigid and trembles in pleasure; I feel an intense pulsing in my entire bottom. It's the best feeling I have ever had, and the pulsing lingers longer than any other orgasm I have experienced. I start to come down from my high when I feel him pull whatever he had near or in my ass out, leaving me feeling empty. That void is quickly filled when he starts pounding me hard with his cock.

I asked him to fuck me hard, and oh my God, he is fucking me hard, and it is awesome. It's so rough, yet it feels so loving. I feel as if Grant and I are more connected now than we've ever been. I can't see him, but I feel his soul and his love for me. His need for me comes out in grunts as he comes, and to my amazement, I come AGAIN! I feel him emptying inside of me as my walls contract around him pumping him for more. He moans loudly as he feels my second orgasm pumping him. "Oh, Shelby, that was … I am not sure I even have words for it. I felt it in my soul, Shelby, did you?" I moan a yes as he takes my blindfold off.

Opening my eyes, I see his eyes gazing into my soul. " I love you so much, and this is what I always knew we could have. Are you okay? Did you enjoy it?"

My eyes tell him everything. He unties my arms, lifts me into his arms, and sets me back on the bed. Going around the room, he blows out all the candles before he comes back to me with a warm washcloth to clean himself from me. He gets into the bed, wraps his strong arms around me, and pulls my body into his.

My back is up against his front, and his entire body is wrapped over mine. It feels so warm and loving.

"I know you, and I know your thoughts almost better than you do. Anything we do together will be loving, erotic, and even if it's rough, it will be tender. One thing it will never be is trashy. I have so much respect for you, but I need you to know just because we do forbidden things in our bed together, it doesn't make you a bad person or a bad mother. It just makes you my sex goddess. Say you will discover the sex goddess within you with me. I know it's in there. I saw it in your eyes when you strutted across that dance floor and demanded I dance with you all those years ago."

I turn over in his arm to see his eyes. We are nose to nose, and I can see him in the moonlight that shines through the window. "That was the most erotic feeling I have ever had, and I look forward to doing more nasty things with you in this bed. I want it to get dirtier by the day." With that statement, I see Grant smile from ear to ear. He pulls me closer to him with my cheek resting on his chest, and he holds me tight until we fall asleep.

Chapter 13

I fall asleep in Grant's arms thinking of how beautiful the night was. Waking a few hours later, I hear the kids already in the kitchen looking for food before school. Grant is still asleep, and we are tangled up in each other. It feels so warm, so close, and oh so nice. My mind starts to wonder about the New Year's Eve party. Is that something we really want to do? We could always go just to see what's going on, right? We wouldn't have to participate. Oh Lord, I hate to admit this, but I think I may need help from my girls.

I try to slip out of the bed without waking him, but that's impossible to do without disturbing our little cocoon. A sleepy-voiced Grant tells me again how much he loves me and wishes we could stay in bed all day. "What a nice thought, but I have to go feed the hungry children in the kitchen, and then we are off to work."

Kissing my forehead, he lets go of me. "Alright, lets go feed the kids."

I text Samantha and Karen to see if they can meet me for Mexican food and margaritas this coming Friday. I let them know I need some individual attention at the restaurant to discuss a previous topic. As usual, Samantha is excited because she just knows it has to be about her sex doctor, but not this time. That girl is nuts; I have to take baby steps, and I am not sure I will ever be ready for her Dr. Love.

Friday takes forever to arrive. We are meeting at our favorite Mexican restaurant, and it is a perfect night to meet. There is a live band playing tonight, and we won't have to whisper to avoid the people at the next table hearing every word we say. I got there early so I could be one drink ahead of the others; I need some liquid courage to get through this. Taking the last sip of my first drink, I see Karen enter the restaurant. I give her a wide smile, and she gives me a sad smile as she scoots into the booth next to me. "Are you okay? It's not like you to drink alone. How bad is it that you need a drink to talk to us?"

"Karen, you know how I am? We have been good friends for a while now, and we've never talked about sex like this. This is just a bit weird for me without being a little loose!" She frowns at me again. "Don't frown at me. I just need to get comfortable because this is a bit out of my comfort zone, okay?"

"I will give you this one, but we are all big girls; we all have sex. It's really no big deal."

My eyes get big as I shake my head. "I know, Karen, but trust me, this is off the charts for us."

"You really think so? You also thought that your husband's top three list was only HIS top three and not the top three of every man on the face of the Earth."

We both bust out laughing because she's right. This may not be that out of the box, but I don't have a clue. Samantha enters the restaurant and walks our way. She waves and smiles at at us from across the room and yells, "You bitches started drinking without me?" Yep, she's nuts. We both hide our faces with our hands pretending she's not with us, as she sits down at our table.

"Come on, girls, the music is so loud no one heard me."

"I'm sure the older couple that rolled their eyes at you heard you just fine."

"Screw them; what ya got? Let's cut to the crap, and tell me if you are going to see Dr. Love or not. That's what this meeting is about, right?"

"No, Samantha, I am not going to see Dr. Love; however, I have another invitation that's just as intriguing, but I need help from ya'll to make the right decision."

"Oh, I've got to hear this. But when you're done, I have a story to tell ya'll. My Great-Aunt Gertrude just gave me some *intriguing* family history that I can't wait to share. So spill it woman; Karen and I don't have all day. We need to get a buzz on and get home to our hubbies. You know, they love it when we get buzzed since they get a good wild night when we get back." Karen slaps at Samantha's hand playfully, trying to get her to shut up. "What? You know it's true. That is the only reason they agree to watch the kids and pick us up so we don't have to drive home drunk."

I lean in closer to the middle of the table. "This is the deal, girls. I went to the sex toy place I told ya'll about near my work."

"Oh yea, I am still a bit mad with you because you wouldn't take me." Samantha pouted.

"Well then, you'll probably be pissed when I tell you what happened to me when I was there. So please hold all outbursts until the end of the story because I may not have it in me to tell it all if you interrupt every two seconds."

Karen and Samantha both listen to my escapade at the

sex shop quietly with non-judging expressions. Once I'm done, I sit back, take a long pull of my drink, and wait for the bomb to go off. But it never does. It appears Samantha knows I need her to be serious and truthful. She leans over the table to where Karen and I sit, and with a wild smile on her face, she quietly says, "I really think this is more your speed. Dr. Love is great, but she's for crazies like me, not you. I know this won't surprise ya'll, but I have been to this type of club before. I have not been to the one in New Orleans, but I have been to one in New York. Phillip and I had a great time. Like I said, you know we are a bit wild, and this was right for us after Dr. Love. We had a great time, and let's just leave it at that."

Karen has not said a word so I'm afraid I am making a mistake by considering it; is she in shock? I knew Samantha would be onboard, or I should say overboard. But if Karen thinks its nuts, then I may have to pass on the idea without even bringing it up to Grant. I look over at Karen, and she seems to be glazed over, in another world. "Karen, hello, anybody home, Karen? Do you think I am nuts? Is this a bad idea? Her eyes finally shift to mine, and she smiles before looking down toward the table.

I barely hear her say, "I have always wanted to do that, but have never told anyone about it." She looks up at me with a flushed face. "If it makes you excited to think about going, then you should go! I have heard that it's very difficult to get into that club."

I let go of the breath I didn't realize I had been holding. "Really, Karen? You think I should go?"

"Hell, yes!" Samantha yells from across the table. What the heck am I over here, chopped liver? Don't you care what I think?"

Karen and I can't do anything but laugh at her. Samantha gets serious again, which always makes me nervous. She motions Karen and I to lean across the table to get closer to her, and she starts to share the rules of the sex club.

"Shelby, you really have to hear what I'm about to tell you, and don't take it lightly. You know I don't usually talk all serious, but I want to make sure you have fun and don't get yourself and Grant into more relationship trouble."

I know where she is going with this, but since she has been to a similar place, I better hear her out.

"I'm sure you have a packet, right?" I nod my head yes as she continues, "Your packet will tell you everything I am telling you, but I want you to understand that it's a big deal. Don't go into it without agreeing to the rules first, or this could end your marriage."

This forces me to take a deep breath, because this is supposed to be helping, not hurting. "Shit, I should pass on this, right? This is not for me?"

"Shelby, get your head out of your ass and listen to me. I'm not telling you this to make you back out. I just want to make sure you enjoy yourself and not hurt your relationship. I'm assuming you don't want to swap partners or add a partner while you're there?"

I don't answer her as I look down at the table.

"Am I correct, Shelby?"

My eyes dance around the room and back down at the table as I nod my head yes.

"Come on, Shelby, I have been to places like that. Don't be embarrassed."

"Yes, you are correct. I just thought it would be sexy to check it out and see what goes on." It's hard to whisper with the loud music playing, but I say the rest in the lowest audible voice I have. "If we have the nerve to do it out there in front of other people, then we can, but won't that be a game-day decision?"

"That's what I thought, Shelby. What you need to do is tell Grant you were invited and that you really want to check it out. Let him know under no circumstances will you swap partners or share either of you. Advise him that you will have to make those intentions clear prior to your visit. You set the rules, and let him know that's what makes you comfortable. Once you choose, you will be given a wrist bracelet that lets everyone there know what your choice is. They wont try to swap with you if you don't have on the correct color bracelet. They will mingle, and the entire atmosphere will be very sultry. The idea is to try and have you change your mind for the next visit. Promise me, Shelby, that you will do this—that you will set the rules whichever way you want them before you go, but don't let anyone push you to do something you are not comfortable doing."

"Yes, I promise."

"Have fun, my girl. You go be the sex kitten I always knew you were under those stuffy clothes."

"Girl, have I ever told you that you are nuts?"

"Ha, yes you have, many times. And I love being nuts because that means I'm not boring."

Karen finally pipes up, "Samantha, boring is something we will never accuse you of being. Now, let's give Shelby a break, and you tell us about your Great-Aunt Gertrude's story."

Chapter 14

"Oh yea … y'all are going to die when you hear this."
My great-aunt is ninety-eight years old and has a mind like a
steel trap. She has not forgotten a thing in her life. I try to
visit her every month, but it's hard sometimes since she
lives in the middle of the French Quarter. Actually, it's not
far from that club you have been invited to." She's looking
at me as she wags her eyebrows trying to be funny. "So,
anyway, because it's forty-five minutes away, and it's such a
pain to park in that area, I don't always make it as often as I
would like. I have to admit, I get my spunk from the old
lady. Everyone else in our family is very stuffy. In old-
people fashion, Aunt Gertrude immediately reminds me
that it has been a month-and-a-half since I last visited. She
asked me to sit at the end of her bed. Like me, she is rarely
serious, so I got very worried. For nighty-eight, she's in
great health, but I don't know how long her body will allow
her to hang on. She pulls an envelope from under her sheet
and tells me she wants to go over her will. She never had
children, and she is not afraid to admit I have always been
her favorite, which is something that everyone in our family
already knows. Even though she was in her late sixties
when I was a teen, I always remember her being very sexy
for her age. My mom would always remark how
inappropriately she dressed for her age, and that she was a
shame to the family because of her past. But no one would
ever say what that meant. When I was old enough to ask
about her past, the subject never came up, so I didn't ask.

Aunt Gertrude decided to tell me about her past yesterday."

Great Aunt Gertrude

"Samantha, you know you have always been my favorite? We are so much alike; unlike the rest of our family, we are fun and full of life. From the time you hit puberty, I always saw myself in you. You were so sexy and confident. I see you starting to blush, but please don't be embarrassed. I'm about to tell you why the family has always been ashamed of me. You can save your blushing for later. Before I tell you, please know I have never been ashamed of my actions. I promised them I would never tell my story in order to save them the embarrassment. But quite frankly, Samantha, at ninety-eight, I really don't give a damn what they think. In this envelope, I have my will. Everything I own I'm giving to you. You have never judged me and have always loved spending time with me. I've always wanted to tell you the truth about me, and you are plenty old enough to hear it.

"I graduated college as a teacher because that's what my parents wanted me to do. I never wanted to be tied down with a husband. I loved men way too much to have only one. Back then that was considered 'shameful.' My parents had a lot of money, and they put me up in this very apartment here in the Quarter. They said if I wanted to act like a whore, I could live with them on Bourbon Street."

"I wasn't too offended by their comments as I never cared what other people thought of me. I have always been a good person, and they couldn't see past what they called the provocative side of me. But to tell you the truth, I was just very sensual. So let me tell you as quickly and painlessly as possible.

"You see, I knew I was not a whore, but the whores were making more money than teachers. It was the mid-forties and the War was over. All the Navy ships stopped here at the Port of New Orleans to restock before moving on to other destinations and bringing our boys back home. There were some good-looking men on those ships. I taught school during the day, but would spend my nights having fun in the Quarter. While having drinks with a sailor from Maine, we wandered into a ... what do you call them today? A strip club? Back then, they were called burlesque shows. I was drawn to their movements, to what they were doing, and how beautiful they looked. It was a true show with dancing and singing, and their costumes were so elaborate, not to mention the amount of money they were pulling in."

"Keep in mind, by then, I was twenty-nine years old and an old maid in those days. Luckily for me, I have always ignored my age. I left my soldier's lap to find the owner of the establishment. Hell, another boat full of soldiers would be in port the next weekend. I found Maxine and told her I wanted at job. She asked me about my experience. I told her, 'I have twenty-four years of dance and thirteen years of sex which makes me more qualified than the eighteen-year-old kids she had up there.'

"Needless to say, I came back in the morning for an audition and got a job. I still taught during the day, but danced on the weekends. I loved it; I was meant to do that. I felt so much power when I was up there. Months later, my parents were killed in a car accident, and as their only child, I received all their money and property. They owned the entire block this apartment sits on. I opened my own club with my newly inherited money and property. They left me enough money to make it a high-class place, not a sleazy club like Maxine was running. You should have seen it! Red velvet sofas, large dazzling chandeliers, and black glossy stages that the girls danced on. I trained my girls to be elegant, and my club was the highest-grossing club in the south. But once all of our boys were home from war, the boring fifties set in. By 1955, I was begging people to visit the club just to stay open.

"I had visited Las Vegas and was invited to an exclusive party there. I won't go into details, but I knew New Orleans' old money would love this type of club. They like to think they have something that poor people don't have or can't be a part of. So I exploited that. Downstairs was the burlesque club, and upstairs was the exclusive club. This was unheard of in the south at the time, so I had to pay off a lot of people. I kept a few of my best girls downstairs with a sexy décor to keep the atmosphere going. But it was never a whorehouse like your mother has always believed it was.

"I charged people an obscene amount to become members, and they did what they wanted to each other while my girls danced in chic birdcages out of reach from the patrons. This lasted through to the mid-sixties until the DA closed the joint down under some bullshit law. The building has been boarded up ever since that day. And now it's your turn to do what you want with it.

"I'm not saying you should do what I did, but if anyone could do it with class, it would be you. And if you rent it out to a church to save all the sinners on Bourbon, I would be fine with that also. I can feel that I only have a little time left, and I just wanted you to know I was fun, sexy, and a legend in my own time. You are the only person I have ever known that would still love me and be proud of me for it."

"Oh, Aunt Gertrude, that's the best history lesson I've ever had. I thank you for including me in your will, and I promise I will give it deep thought before I make any decisions. But please tell me you have pictures from the past to add to my imagination."

With a smile, she said, "Well, of course, I do, dear. I knew you would have a positive reaction. Go to the wardrobe, open the long mirror, and pull out the large tin box. All my photos and news clippings from that time are in that box. There are also some diaries you can read, once I'm gone."

Samantha sits back and lets us take in her story. "Aunt Gertrude and I had a great time going through that box and bringing her back to her younger years. She was a fox." Karen and I are both sitting there with our mouths hanging wide open. We just look at each other in utter shock.

"Did you just make that shit up? This is too ironic that your aunt is speaking to you about a sex club when I have an invitation to one."

"You know I believe in signs. This is your sign to go for it. Now, let's get the hell out of here. All this talk about sex has me horny! I texted Phillip to pick us up about ten minutes ago. Let's go wait outside."

Chapter 15

Now, how to tell Grant? I feel as if I'm in the middle of a transition; a caterpillar turning into a butterfly. I'm not quite ready to fly, but I want to break out of this cocoon. The sex goddess within me has been awakened. I have daily thoughts of making love to Grant. I find myself thinking of ways to sexually surprise him or trying to think of what we can do that will be exciting, even at work. I think of what I can buy to wear under winter outfits that will drive him crazy as we sit at the kids' games or at dinner.

Yet with all that going on in my head, I'm still too shy to tell him it's there. I want to break that habit. I am almost forty years old, and I have been married for twenty years. There's nothing to hide from him; this is it, and this is us! It's official. I am breaking free of my cocoon and flying like the beautiful butterfly I know I can be.

I make some calls and arrange for the kids to spend Saturday night away from home. I make reservations at Ruby Reds, a historic steak house, in New Orleans. This place is a small hole in the wall with the best steaks around. I requested a booth so we would be able to sit very close without others hearing our conversation. They also have long white tablecloths. Yep, no one can see what's going on under the table.

The dress there is casual. Grant is in jeans and a polo shirt, and I decide on a maxi dress with a sweater and knee-high leather boots. November down south is beautiful. Our fall has dry and cool weather. Did I happen to mention I left my panties at home?

We were seated in the back of the room in a booth just as I requested. Ruby's is romantically lit with red candleholders on each table. We sip wine and talk while we wait for our dinner. Grant wraps his arm around me, and I am pressed against his chest with my arm around his waist. He lifts my chin so he can look into my eyes. "Thank you for not leaving me. Thank you for forgiving me and sticking it out." He leans down and kisses me firmly.

We are interrupted by the noise of our dinner plates placed on the table. The food smells delicious. His words have distracted me a bit from my original plan. I let Grant get halfway through his meal before my hand slides up his thigh to caress his soft penis. I really should have waited until he was done chewing! I thought I was going to have to do the Heimlich maneuver on him. Now, the entire restaurant is watching and making sure he is still breathing. So much for sexy stroking under the table. We are both laughing hysterically now. After we calm down, we both start eating again, and I slide my hand back up his thigh. He's not so surprised this time, and he opens his legs a bit to give me better access. My hand slides up his jeans and over his bulge; I can feel his hardness now! I start to rub up and down his length with my left hand while I casually eat with my right.

It's difficult to carry a normal conversation, but we manage. The waiter comes back to collect our dishes. "Would you all like dessert?" Under the table, Grant puts his large hand over mine to still my motions; he is close to coming in his pants. I don't typically order dessert, and I know Grant is ready to get out of here, but he has not felt the real surprise yet.

"I will have crème brûlée, and my husband would love some bread pudding." When the waiter walks away, I don't say a word to Grant. I simply lift my leg across his lap and direct his hand up my thigh.

It doesn't take him long to figure out what I want. His eyes give me a questioning look to make sure. I lean over and whisper in his ear, "I want you to fuck me with your fingers right here and make me come with all these people sitting in this restaurant."

"Oh, Shelby, that's so hot; you are so fucking sexy I may come in my pants."

I whisper to him, "That's okay with me."

I feel his hand at my knee sliding over my suede boots. He gently rubs and massages all the way up to my inner thigh. The waiter approaches our table again to ask if we would like more wine, which I graciously accept for myself. Grant has to drive back home, so he will have to make do with only dessert. He decides to test my limits as the waiter is pouring my wine. he slides his fingers right into my slit, expecting to find panties. I could tell by the look on his face that he was the one surprised. I give him a quick grin as I thank the waiter. The waiter is almost done picking up our dinner plates when Grant's fingers slide out of me, then up and down my wet lips to my clit.

As soon as the waiter walks away, he leans over to me and says, "You are so wet for me. How am I going to stop myself from fucking you on this table?"

I give an innocent sexy shoulder shrug. "I don't know, but please make me come soon."

Waiting for our dessert, Grant teases my clit and gingerly slides his fingers in and out of my slit. I am so close. It's so raunchy to do this in front of everyone, but it makes it feel that much better, and no one seems to notice. Once our dessert arrives, I start to sample it. The crème brûlée is so good combined with the motion in between my legs. I truly feel like Meg Ryan in that movie. With an intense stare, he watches my face carefully while I eat with his two fingers slowly gliding in and out of me and his thumb circling my clit. This is too intense. I am coming, and I don't know how not to scream. I put my head down in my palm as if I'm laughing and let my release take over. Once I recover, Grant lifts his hand from under the table and licks his fingers. "That's the best dessert I've ever had." This was such an arousing experience.

We pay the bill and head home. I figure the forty-minute drive home will be a good time to tell him about the party.

Chapter 16

"Did you enjoy your dinner?"

"Oh, you know I did. Did it turn you on to do that in public?"

"You were sitting at the table with me; is it necessary to ask that question?" He smiles as I go on, "I have to admit, it was a bit awkward at first, but yes, after the initial shock wore off, it was very exciting." I watch his body language as he drives. I still sense he's a bit nervous or uncomfortable about the incident. "Was it a great one-time thing, or would you want to do that again?" And here it comes. I can tell by his face that it's not something he wants to do again. The party's not going to be a good idea. He is clearly conflicted by what he wants to say. I see the creased lines in his forehead as he rubs it. This is my sign that he has something to say that he really doesn't want to say out loud.

He glances over at me from the wheel with a very concerned look. "I'm really concerned that you are doing things to try and be bold and sexy because of the "incident." I feel like I'm forcing you to go out of the box, to do things you wouldn't normally do. I don't want to be that man. I don't want to be the husband you hate because I made you do things that you believe are immoral, things that disgust you. I love you no matter what, and it would break my heart if you were doing these things just because you thought I'd leave if you don't. I'm not going anywhere. I love you and will be with you forever. I made a huge mistake, and it will never happen again. It's one thing to do a little more in the bedroom, but I don't want to push you this far if it's not something you want to do on your own. I really have been concerned that you are going overboard just to please me. Don't get me wrong, I love it; I love the new sensual side of you. It's un-freaking-believable. But I want you to do it only if it's what comes natural to you. If that's what you want to do."

Oh, how I love that he's so concerned about me. It fills my heart with joy that he truly loves me this much that he's upset I may be doing this against my better judgment. "So, are you saying that scene at the restaurant was too intense for you to handle?"

"God, no, Shelby, I loved it! I just want to make sure you wanted to do it. I am sorry to make a big deal about it, but this is so unlike you. Twenty years ago, this is what I would have thought you would have turned out to be, but after the kids, it was just different. Your sexuality did not grow after that."

"I understand where you're coming from, but please know that while our "cyber incident" was, and still can be, very painful, I've learned from it. I've grown more than I could have ever imagined. We should want to be like this when we are sixty and eighty. We are all we have left at the end of the day. Our kids will grow up and leave us; we need to want to be together. I have discovered something from within myself that I did not know existed, and it is beautiful." I scoot over in the seat, lean up against him, and rub my hand up and down along his hard length, "Do you want me to spread my wings, Grant? I have so much more in store for us, but I need to know that you know I am doing it for me, for us, and because I want to go on a sexual journey with you. Do you want to go on that journey with me, Grant?"

"I will go anywhere with you, Shelby, just tell me when and where, and I will be there."

I nuzzle my nose on the side of his check while I rub his now rock-hard cock. I lick the outside of his ear. "Anywhere?"

"Yes, Shelby, anywhere; where do you want to go?"

" I want to go to a New Year's Eve party in the French Quarter."

"That sounds like fun. Of course, we can do that. Is it at a club or a hotel? What's the name of the place?"

"It's called Savannah's Closet."

"I have never heard of that place."

"Well, now that you understand that I'm breaking out of my cocoon and am willing to do some out of the box things, understand this is one of them. Remember the silk tie set I bought you for our anniversary?"

"Of course, I do. I still dream about it. We have to make a habit of using them more often."

"We will, I promise. But first, let me explain. When I bought them, the saleslady had asked me a ton of questions, and she felt like we were candidates to be invited to this party. She only had a few invitations to give, and she thought we needed this. I know, what does the lady at the sex shop know? Apparently, she could be a sex therapist because she was dead on. Anyway, this is a sex club." I pause and wait for his reaction while still gently stroking his cock as we talk. His eyes get big, but he doesn't take them off the road. He is getting harder, so I know it's a turn on for him.

"Did you just say what I thought you did?"

"Yes, I did. Now, don't get too excited because in no way do I want to be swingers. This is a swingers club, but the website says straight couples are welcome. I just thought it would be seductive to go and see where it takes us. I'm not sure I would be able to have sex in front of other people, but I think it would be interesting to see what goes on there. I have the packet at home, and we have to go over a few things to make sure we have our own ground rules before we go. Tell me, Grant, are you in, or do you want to think about it first?"

"Think? Hell, no, there's no thinking required. I'm in. But I have to admit, I'm not down with the swinging stuff either. I would never want to see you with another man. Now, another woman, that I might be able to do! But I could also do without it, so don't feel like that's something you have to check off your list."

"I understand, and I have to admit I am not sure about that either. Don't tell anyone, but Samantha and her Phillip have done it with another woman, and she said it was the best experience they ever had." His eyes come off the road for a split second to glance over at me.

"Are you are shitting me? Did they really? What the heck? Did they hire a hooker?"

I giggle. "No, they did not hire a hooker." Then I tell him the whole Dr. Love story.

"What I'm saying is, I don't want to rule it out, but I don't want to promise it to you either. Let's go home and look at the paperwork, and we can decide what we want to do."

"Paperwork, there's paperwork for this party?"

"Yep, we have to decide if we are only going to be with each other, share with anyone, or only share girl-on-girl." I'm glad to see we are nearing the end of the twenty-three-mile bridge; it is a miracle he has not gotten a ticket during our little talk. The last time I checked, he was doing ninety in a sixty-five.

"You need to slow down; we will be home soon enough, and I will show you the packet. If we want to have sex with each other or even give oral sex to each other, we need to be tested by their doctors. I know it's kind of weird, but those are the rules. Once we decide what we want, we will go to the doctor. After it's all approved, they will send us ID badges and bracelets in the mail. The badges will have all the color codes on the back so no one tries to approach you in a manner in which you are not comfortable with."

"So, are you saying if we do just each other, we cant speak to anyone else?"

"No, we can socialize with anyone, but they don't want you to make unwanted advances to someone that has stated via their bracelet they are not interested. And changing your mind on the premises is not allowed; that means if I say no to girl-on-girl before we go and I change my mind once I'm there, too bad, so sad."

"I have to admit ,I am not sure if we are ready for that. I know it's my number one fantasy, but now that it's a real possibility, I'm not sure if I want to make you do that."

"That makes two of us. I am not sure about it either.

But I'm sure about the party, are you?"

"Yes, can you feel how hard my dick is in your hand? That should tell you, I'm sure." With a smile on my face, I kiss his cheek and pull away to my side of the truck. We are now pulling into our subdivision, ready to run each other over to get to the bedroom. This is going to be hard and quick since the foreplay has lasted three hours.

We literally run to the front step where Grant is trying his best to get the key into the door. Barely inside the door, I'm tugging at Grant's zipper then dropping to my knees and taking him into my mouth. I slide my tongue around the tip and up and down the shaft. As much as I want him inside of me right now, I'm being greedy. Sucking him makes him very large and hard. I want to get him as big as possible. Taking him deep into my throat, I suck as I pull out. I only get a few sucks in before Grant has scooped me up and gathered my dress around my waist. He lifts me by my ass, and I wrap my legs around his waist. I feel my back pressed up against the front door.

"Hold onto my neck; this is going to be quick."

I wrap my arms around his neck and hold on tight as his huge dick is at my entrance. He's rubbing it up and down my wetness. I am about to beg for it when he pushes in with one hard thrust. His pelvic bone is up against mine with his balls on my ass. It's so deep in this position. He pins me up against the door with his shoulders and he grabs my thighs to hold me up as he pounds in and out of me. I feel the tingling in my toes that comes just before my orgasm. I lift my pelvis to give him more of me, and he takes it, all of it; we are both moaning and panting. He picks up his pace, and I know he's close. I let go and allow my release to hit me in all its glory. My body shakes with pleasure while Grant is still pumping in and out. Within seconds, he is coming right behind me calling out my name in between hard kisses.

Chapter 17

Well, that went well! The whole sex club thing and the hands-on attention at Ruby Reds pleasantly surprised Grant. This is going to be exciting. But what is not exciting is this verification process.

We completed the first part of the application, which was basic information to make sure we're not criminals or law enforcement. I'm not sure which one is worse to them. Anyway, now we sit in their private doctor's office. This is a fancy office in the ritzy uptown area. This exam includes a basic health test to make sure your heart can withstand a lot of excitement! There is a blood test to make sure we don't have STDs and a saliva test to check our hormone levels. If our hormone levels are low, this document states they will offer us supplements to take the week before the party.

While the entire ordeal is awkward, it also gives us a sense of comfort knowing the level of concern in reference to passing diseases from person to person. Our exam is done, and we are waiting for our paperwork when a very attractive redheaded woman walks in. She doesn't say a word to us but smiles in a very knowing way, which makes me blush.

Before now, we were the only patients in the waiting room. Suddenly, the room feels cramped, and I'm ready to bolt. The redhead puts her name on the clipboard and sits next to me. The entire room is empty, and she takes the freaking seat next to me as I try my best to ignore the situation. Just as she sits down, the door opens, a nurse steps out, hands me paperwork, and with a polite smile, says, "You two are all set; have a good time at Savannah's Closet."

That's my cue to get the heck out of Dodge. I bend down to pick up my purse, and when I start to stand, I feel a slender hand on my arm. I turn to see the redhead who says, "I sure hope to see you at the party wearing a pink bracelet."

I simply smile and walk away. OMG, I'm not sure if I can do this. I'm having a bit of a mini panic attack as we walk out to the parking lot. Grant notices my frozen face. "What did she say to you?"

I tell him what she said, and we have a repeat of the same conversation we had on the bridge the night of our dinner at Ruby's. "I know, I know, I don't have to do this, and I just might not. Let me think about it, please. We have until mid-December to pick a bracelet, which gives me nine days left to decide." Nine days to decide if I even want to go, at this point! Good thing we didn't have to pay the $500.00 invitation fee in addition to the $300.00 per person doctor's fee. I have nothing holding me to this party if I change my mind. I just have to decide in NINE days.

Eight days have gone by, and I have changed my mind back and forth a million times. It's the old boring me fighting my new inner sex goddess. I want to let the sex goddess win, I really do, but can I let her win? Yes, yes, I can. We are going to the party, and I have chosen to wear a pink bracelet. What does pink mean, you ask? Yep, it means that I can mingle with the ladies if I choose. Grant has a black bracelet which means he can only mingle with me. Even though I have gone back and forth, I decide to give myself the option if I want it. I know Grant won't push me, so I want to have the option if I feel like it's something for us.

All the paperwork has been completed, arrangements have been made for the kids, and we are all set. I have one more surprise up my sleeve—a limo—yep, limo sex!

We have received our password and additional information to access the club's member's only site. I received the e-mail earlier today at work, and it is killing me not to look, but I'm certain the site is blocked by corporate. Grant and I wait for the kids to go to bed before checking it out. We log on to the website, and it has tons of pictures, none of which are during business hours. It appears they were taken before they were open for business. We are still able to get an idea of what to expect when we get there, or at least the layout of the club, anyway. I'm glad to see it appears clean. For the money people spend to go to this place, I would have imagined it would be a bit fancier. But on a scale of one to ten, I would call it a seven.

Just as Candy explained, they have two floors to the club. The first floor is the introduction level, where people can get to know each other, called the Ballroom. This is a clothing-required floor. Their New Year's Eve theme is Masquerades. Typical New Orleans style black tie for men, formal gowns for women, and masks, which are required for everyone on the first floor, per the website. The pictures we scroll through online show the ballroom to be a typically classy bar setting. There is a large marbled dance floor and a bar on one end with a piano off to the other side.

The second floor is where all the action takes place. From the pictures, half appears to be a lounging area with separated seating spaces. The walls are covered in large canvas prints of men and women in different provocative poses. We come across one picture that shows beds lined up on the far wall with sheer curtains as barriers. Flipping around the site, we come to the conclusion that the pictures are a description of what that area is used for. I'm both panicked and aroused. It's a very strange mix of emotions. It's amazing how much a person can know your thoughts without a word being said.

Grant starts to rub the back of my shoulders as he senses my discomfort. "We're going to have a great time; if we hate it, we will simply leave. But, who else do you know OTHER than Samantha that can say they have been to a place like this?" Reaching over, he gently turns my face to him and gazes into my eyes. "Trust me. Trust me to take care of you when we're there, to take care of your needs and your fears; I wont let you down."

My anxiety evaporates instantly. "I love you so much. I promise to let you take care of me." I lean forward, surrendering my lips to him. Pushing his hand through my hair to the nape of my neck, he makes a closed fist and firmly pulls my head back as he starts to explore my mouth. The force he uses is surprising; this is not his nature, but it feels good to give him control again. I feel him smile against my lips. Lowering his head, he takes a nip at my ear. "Let's go to bed, Bossy Girl."

"You are calling me bossy right now? Because at this moment, I don't feel like I'm in control. Not that I don't enjoy it, but you seem to be the boss at the moment."

"Shelby, you know just as much as I do, you are always in control. You liked me pulling your hair? Didn't you?" I nod my head yes. "Now, let's get that ass of yours to bed and see if you'll let me get a few spanks in for being a bad girl."

We head off to bed and have another steamy night. A night that we can say, "That night was one of the best nights we have ever had!" I want to be able to say that every time we make love. I want to be able to say, "That was the most erotic thing I have ever done!"

Chapter 18

Time to hit the mall; I need a gown, shoes, and thigh-highs, of course! I decide to check out the ball gown section first to see if there is anything that would be sexy enough for the party. A young saleswoman introduces herself as Meg and asks, "What can I help you find today?" If only this poor girl knew. I decide to keep most details to myself and tell her I need a formal floor-length gown that can possibly break down to a cocktail dress for a masquerade ball.

Meg claps her hands in excitement. "I have the perfect dress for you. It comes in two colors—black for a sleek sexy look or royal purple for a glamorous look. Both are trimmed in gold embroidery with beading work that makes the bodice sparkle." She grabs my hand like we are teenage BFFs and pulls me across the department store to where all the formal Mardi Gras gowns are located. She rounds the rack and pulls the royal purple gown out first. It's breathtaking and exactly what I asked her for. The bodice is a fitted corset with a deep plunging sweetheart neckline adorned with sparkling beads and embroidered gold filigree. The skirt is reminiscent of *Gone with the Wind*, and the bottom is big and puffy with lots of silk fabric that billows down to the ground. There's a wide purple ribbon around the waist and a large fabric rose in the back with two long ribbons hanging perfectly behind the dress. I look up at Meg in amazement that she has instantly found the exact dress I described to her and in my favorite color.

And she knows it, I can tell by the smile on her face as she goes on, "Wait for it, I have more. Did you forget about the cocktail dress?" I smile and nod my head yes; I was so taken by the dress I totally forgot about my second request. She pulls a button from behind the rose, and the skirt drops to the floor. There is a fitted cocktail-length skirt underneath that is the same color as the long skirt, but fitted with a gold scallop trim. It's not as short as I would like, but being the Holly the Homemaker that I am, I know I can fix that quickly on my sewing machine at home.

I head to the dressing room to try it on, and Meg comes along. "This dress is a two-person job and, you will need my help." She is right; this dress is so heavy, I will need Grant to help me in and out of it.

Once Meg strings me up, I turn to the mirror. "WOW," is all I can say. The royal purple reminds me of the satin ties Grant and I used the night of our anniversary. The gold beads and embroidery are absolutely gorgeous, so detailed and elegant. This dress has a price tag of $1,100.00, but lucky me, it's on clearance for $350.00 due to a stain at the bottom of the cocktail dress in the back. Since I'm cutting that off anyway, it's a great deal for me. And I think we will just have to buy tickets to the Endymion Ball next Mardi Gras! Karen has been begging us for years to go to the ball with her, as her husband rides in the parade every year. Meg can tell by how great this dress looks on me that she has made a sale. I blurt out, "I say yes to the dress, Meg. Ring me up. I have more shopping to do."

After purchasing the dress, I head over to the undergarment section. Meg will hold onto the dress until I return. She wants to see the shoes I buy before leaving, and the dress is too heavy to lug around the store anyway. I'm unsure of what color thigh-highs to buy. Black is too dark and nude has no pizazz. I am starting to get discouraged as I wander from store to store. Finally, I find something that would look magnificent once the floor length skirt is removed. The tops of the stockings are a beautiful gold lace, and the stockings themselves are a sheer shimmering gold. Oh so sexy. Stockings, check, and now, off to find shoes!

I head back to the department store and down the escalator to the shoe department. Gold shoes are a must, but it will be tricky to find a classy pair. It must be my lucky day today. I come across another great sale. I see a pair of Dolce & Gabbana in my size. They are 75% off and stunning. I'm not one to wear super high heels, but these have a three-inch platform to go with the five-inch spiked heel. The heels are a shiny gold metal, and it reminds me of a bullet. The actual shoe is a gold shimmery material covered in gold sequins that fan out from the top to the bottom of the peep-toe. They are very movie star looking. Since the platform offsets the height, I tell myself they will be manageable to walk in for a few hours. And for $30.00, who cares if I never wear them again.

I head back up the escalator to find Meg and my dress. She sees me coming from across the store and lights up with excitement. "What did you get?" she calls out from across the store. I look around to notice there is no one else around; I must be the highlight of her day. Laughing as

I approach her, I pull out the shoes.

In a very dramatic voice, she says, "OMG, these shoes were made for this dress. You are going to look so freaking hot, your husband is going to think he died and went to heaven."

"Thanks, I really appreciate your help. I couldn't have done this without you. I'll be sure to recommend all my friends to you personally." She smiles and gives me a hug. "Have a great time at the ball, Cinderella." I head out of the door with my big heavy dress and other bags. It's a struggle to make it to the car, but thankfully, I was parked close to the door.

Chapter 19

The most anticipated day of our marriage has arrived. I'm trying to pack my suitcase as we booked a hotel room in the city for a mini vacation. I have to admit, my nerves are back. The kids have already headed off to their destinations, and with one hour before the limo gets here, my stomach starts to turn. I'm not sure if I can do this. Can I do this? Have I been kidding myself with all the smut reading? Believing I have the balls to do this? Let's throw out the girl-on-girl stuff for a moment; right now, that's so far from possible, I'm not even sure I can walk out of the front door.

Grant has stepped out of the bathroom into the bedroom wrapped in a towel. I don't even notice him until he is pressed up against my back with his warm breath on the back of my neck. "You don't have to do this if you don't want, but I know you can. I'll be right there with you. I won't leave you for a second. Not one second. Whatever you want to do is fine with me."

I turn into his arms, rest my cheek on his chest, and run my fingers though the soft hair covering his chest. Just having him this close saying those words helps wash away my fears. I look up into his handsome face and find trust; I'm back to where we were before the "cyber incident." I trust Grant with my life, my soul, and my heart.

"Thanks, I really needed that. Now, I have a surprise for you."

His lips turn up in a sexy smile. "I'm not sure my heart

can take any more surprises, Bossy Girl. The last five months have been full of surprises. What could you possibly have left?"

"Just one small surprise; it will arrive in an hour to bring us to the hotel." I raise one eyebrow, and with a half-cocked smile, I say, "A limo!"

His eyes don't leave mine. His smile is controlled as he leans down close to my lips and with a deeper than normal sexy voice, he says, "Are you telling me we are going to have limo sex?"

I giggle at his attempt to be extra sexy. "Yes, that's exactly what I'm telling you. So make sure you save all your testosterone, you are going to need it tonight." I kiss him quickly and continue packing as I shoo him off to do the same.

I make a point of letting him see me put my dress on without panties. I slip on a pair of ballet slippers and a light sweater. December in New Orleans can be anywhere from eight degrees to thirty degrees, but today we are still in the sixties. So it's comfy and cool for us, but not cold. The rest of the hour goes by quickly getting the formal clothes together and making sure I do not forget any essentials: flat iron, curling iron, makeup, and last but not least, my thigh-highs.

Grant and I try not to make eye contact for fear we may jump each other before we leave. We want to make sure we can use the limo for its intended use. Our bags are ready and waiting at the door when my cell phone rings. It's the limo driver; he's going to be about fifteen minutes late. I give Grant a disappointed look. "I just want to be on our way already. The driver is running late. I need a glass of wine to take the edge off. You want one?"

We both have a glass of wine, which works wonders on my nerves. We are primed and ready for the ride; my inhibitions have been tempered for the moment. The limo driver arrives and packs all of our belongings into the trunk. We take the rest of our wine for the ride.

It will take about an hour to go from our home to the hotel in New Orleans. This trip will take us over the longest bridge over water in the world. A glorious twenty-three straight miles over Lake Pontchartrain. There are no stop signs, no red lights, and only two lanes of traffic moving south at sixty-five miles per hour. It's still light out right now, but the tint on the windows is dark enough that no one will be able to see in. By the time we make it to the bridge, it should be dusk. Did I mention I was an over-planner? I tell myself to take a deep breath and take another sip of wine.

I decide to listen to my inner sex goddess and slide into the limo. I don't slide over too far, wanting him right up against my body. He gets in after having a chat with the driver. I don't even ask what has been said; I don't want to know. I'm going to listen to my sex goddess and go with the flow. I'm trying my best not to over-analyze it.

As Grant gets into the car, he leans over to me, hooks his index finger under my chin, and pulls me into a kiss. It's strong and loving, and his tongue is deep and claiming, oh so good. I moan against his lips as he opens his eyes to watch me with his sexy grin. He pulls his lips from mine, and I put my fingers through his hair pulling him back to me for my turn at the wheel. He lets me take control. I lightly slip my tongue through his lips, then retreat, and lick them slowly. I enter his mouth again for a slow dance pulling his tongue into my mouth as if I am giving it a blowjob. I know he loves this; he loves to visualize me sucking him off.

Speaking of a blowjob, that's exactly what's on the agenda next. I know I said no plan, but this is a given! I try to slide down to the floor, but Grant grabs me by the arms and shakes his head no.

"No, ma'am, I'm taking care of you this entire trip." His strong arms pull me over onto the long seat. I'm now flat on my back with Grant on top of me, and my dress is up and over my head. He spreads my legs as far as they will go and gently licks my folds. He licks me slowly from the bottom of my entrance to the top of my clit, stopping there to make slow circles. At this rate, I may come before we exit our subdivision.

I hear Air Supply come through the speakers and give Grant a sideways grin. "Is that what you were chatting to the driver about?" He shrugs his shoulders and looks back down at my wet pussy. I'm soaked already, begging him to fuck me. Grant chuckles. "Sorry, Bossy Girl, you won't get your way this time. We have a long ride. You are going to come more times than you can imagine tonight, so be patient."

He thrusts two fingers into me and it's sheer pleasure. He's moves them in and out while suckling my clit. The feeling is so intense as he has one finger circling my forbidden pucker below. He has not entered it, but just the feeling of him making circles there sends me over the edge. My first orgasm hits me with intense pleasure, and he groans as I explode.

He lets me recover by pulling out of me gently, but he is still softly lapping up my arousal. Once my breathing has leveled out, he pulls his pants off, picks me up by the hips, and turns me around onto his lap. My back is to his front, and he puts me down hard on cock. I gasp in surprise at the roughness, but it feels so deep.

"Ride me, Shelby!"

I plant my feet on the floor and use my yoga-toned muscles to push my body up and down his engorged length. I use long slow strides, feeling his entire cock slide fully in and out of me. I feel the mushroom top and all the veins on the way down. After a few slow strokes, I hear Grant moaning in pleasure as his cock continues to grow larger and stiffer.

I see my very well-prepared purse just within reach and pull out a small hand towel to toss to Grant. With a laugh, he says, "Always a boy scout, Shelby, but I'm far from ready. Keep riding me; it feels so fucking good, I hope I never come." This position allows me to hold myself up with my arms and grind my pelvis around him in a circle.

He has not pushed the envelope too far, but he always leaves me wanting more. I have put my hands on the floor with my ass exposed to him as I grind. Tilting my head to look over my shoulder, I watch him. He licks his thumb and rubs it over my anus. The anticipation makes my pussy throb. I never know if he is going to just massage it or push in. I close my eyes and relax, letting him do as he pleases. I am riding him up and down when I feel his fingertip enter my ass. He lets his rhythm follow mine by pushing in and out at the same time I pull on and off him. I come hard and strong, feeling Grant come right behind me.

I sit back in a hypnotic daze as he wraps me in his arms. "Limo sex is the bomb; we have to do this more often." I hand him the towel as I rise off of him so we can get cleaned up. I sit back onto his lap with him leaning against the side glass to cradle me. We hold onto each other like we have all day as the miles pass by on the bridge. But Grant is not done with me, and to tell you the truth, I want more. My core needs him back inside of me.

My head is still resting on his shoulder as he slips his hand inside the top of my dress and pulls down my bra to expose my breasts. Rubbing them with the right amount of pressure, he rolls one of my erect nipples and sends an electric charge straight down to my pussy. A breathy moan escapes me as I feel the pressure starting to build within myself. He leans his head over and sucks my other nipple into his mouth while continuing to roll and tug the other. The sensation is incredible. Needing to be bare to him, I lift my dress off over my head. Bringing my hands down, I glide them over my belly and my hips in a dramatic fashion. Slowly, my fingers reach my clit, and I slide them up and down my slit. Grant lets out a growl as his eyes roll back in ecstasy. I make a show of my long fingers gliding up and down my lips. The pressure of his tugs on my nipples increases with the motions of my fingers. I dip my middle finger deep down into my pussy, and Grant comes unglued. The suction and pulling he's doing to my nipples has a painful bite followed by extreme pleasure. I pick up the pace of fucking myself, adding my thumb to my clit. I really think Grant may come in his pants; at this point, his moaning and groaning is louder than mine. It's all so carnal—the sounds coming from Grant, the feeling of his mouth, the smell of sex in the air, and my fingers inside myself. It's so beautiful that we have come this far. It makes a tear slip from my eye as I come. Grant licks it from my face with a smile since he knows it's a tear of joy.

"You are so beautiful when you make yourself come. Do you know how hard that makes me? Do you?"

"Oh, yes, I do know how hard it makes you. That's the reason I do it; I am a greedy girl." I smile up at him. "We only have about fifteen minutes left, so please put that hard dick in me." We steam up the limo the rest of the ride there and barely have enough time to put ourselves back together before the driver opens the door.

We have arrived at our hotel, which sits right across the street from the club. After checking into this beautiful old world hotel, we decide to take a little nap before it's time to get ready. We lie in bed together as one in a warm cocoon.

Chapter 20

I pull my hair up in a neat French twist with a few stray curls hanging around my face and in the back. My face is done up with smoky eyes and glossy lipstick. I smooth on the gold thigh-high stockings and attach them to the purple lace garter belt I have on. Looking at my legs in the mirror, I see how far I have come in five months. My legs are toned, my belly is flatter, and my arms actually have a nice shape to them. I smile at my reflection feeling more confident than I have in a long time. With only my garter belt, thigh highs, and heels on, I stand with my hand on my hip and call to Grant. "Hey, I need your help in here, please."

He walks into the bathroom, stops in the doorway, stands against the doorframe in his tux, and glares at me. I intended for him to be taken back by the view, but I'm the one stunned. It has been twenty years since I've seen him in a tux, and he looks just as handsome as he did back then. His tux is black with a royal purple bowtie and vest. I feel like we are going to the prom we never had together. I smile back at him, standing with my corset in hand, dressed only in stockings, garter belt, and heels.

"Are you going to stand there all night and stare or help me into my dress?"

"Do you know how sexy you look, Shelby? I could stand here and look at your naked body all day. I'm not sure I will be able to make it all night knowing what you have on under your dress; you're definitely testing my will tonight, woman."

With a smile, I turn around and step into the loosened corset with attached skirt. The original skirt was knee length with a stain on the back. I removed the beautiful trim along the edge and cut it short enough to remove the stain and to expose the straps of my thigh highs. I also pulled it in a bit to make sure it fit me snugly.

Meg had already tied me up in the corset so Grant didn't have to string it up, and he only had to tighten it. "All done; what's next? Where are your panties?" He looks around the bathroom, but there is no clothing left in the room except for the full skirt to wrap around my waist.

"Why in the world would I waste my time with panties at a sex club, Grant?"

"Oh Lord, I'm not sure I will be able to walk straight knowing your beautiful bare pussy lies under that dress with no barrier. I mean, really, you must be trying to give me a heart attack."

"You'll be fine; help me get this skirt on." He holds my hand as I step into the large ball gown, making sure I don't fall over in these heels. Walking over to my cosmetic bag, I give my neck a few spritzes of perfume and feel Grant's gaze still on me. Looking up into his eyes, I ask, "How do I look?"

He doesn't say a word as he walks over to me, never taking his eyes off mine. When he reaches me, he holds my face in his hands. "You look more beautiful everyday I wake up to you." Leaning his head down, he kisses a soft kiss on the tip of my nose. "Let me put your necklace on." He drapes the gold necklace around my neck, clasps it in the back, and runs his hands over my shoulders down to my hands. The sweetness gives me goose bumps.

Turning around into his arms, I'm now eye-to-eye with him in these heels. His eyes allow me to read his thoughts. "I love you too; let's go put our bracelets and masks on, and we can head to the party." Grabbing his hand, I lead him out of the bathroom to the antique dresser and open the drawer. I have not told him what color bracelet I have chosen. He hasn't pressured me by asking, nor has he tried to persuade me one way or the other. I pull out a large red velvet box and hand him his mask. His is a simple black velvet mask with gold rope trim and a tie to keep it secure.

My mask, of course, is very fancy. It's the exact royal purple of my dress trimmed in Grant's matching gold rope with purple and gold feathers that plume above my head on one side. This mask has thin gold arms similar to sunglasses so I don't have to tie anything around my up-do. I'm sure in any other city we would look out of place walking out of a hotel room dressed like this, but not in New Orleans! Masquerade parties are held year round, and it's not uncommon in the French Quarter to see people dressed in formal wear with Mardi Gras masks in any given month.

Right before we head out the door, I open the white box our bracelets arrived in. They are silver chain bracelets with a round quarter-sized tag on each of them. Grant's bracelet is clearly for a man as it has larger links, and mine is more feminine and dainty. I put Grant's bracelet on his wrist, and his black tag can clearly be seen from under his tux as it hangs down low onto his hand.

His eyes grow large when I hand him my bracelet to put on me. My bracelet has a large PINK tag on it.

"This is going to be a very exciting night. I love you so much. Don't ever forget that." Pulling me in by my waist, he leans me over and dips me as if we were ballroom dancing, kissing me passionately. I was unsure how he would react to the pink tag, but he throws me a curve ball by ignoring the color altogether.

"I'm glad you wore that smudge-proof lipstick tonight. I plan on kissing you all night and would hate to smudge those sexy lips."

"Let's go, handsome." We step out of the elevator into the old world French lobby. Everyone turns and watches as we walk by. We get nods and smiles as if we are movie stars. I hear an older women say, "What a stunning couple." We both look at each other and smile, knowing these people have no idea where we're going and what we're about to do. They assume we are going to a simple black-tie New Year's Eve party.

I had grabbed my gold clutch on the way out of the door with our ID badges, touch-up makeup, and personal wipes for clean up. What? I can't help it I am an over-planner. Grant had grabbed two bottles of wine since the club does not serve alcohol and has a bring your own liquor policy. They label it and serve it back to you with a corking charge.

The hotel is right across the street from the club. It's not far to walk, but I'm sure on the way back, I'll be wearing my ballerina slippers I also stuffed into my clutch.

We are now standing on the front steps of the club. There's nothing on the door other than the address. There is no way anyone else would know there is a business behind this door. Grant looks at me before we move forward. "Are you sure you want to do this? I will love you and have fun with you in that gown no matter what! It's your call." I don't respond to him verbally and push him toward the door. He turns the knob, and we enter into a small lobby with a bouncer of sorts waiting with a smart phone in his hand. He doesn't smile at us; he simply looks up and says in a scary deep voice, "ID Badge!"

I hand over the cards to him, and once they are scanned and confirmed, he smiles and properly greets us as he opens the locked door behind him, "Please enjoy your evening at Savannah's Closet." Grant holds the door open as I enter. There's a long hallway that leads to the main floor as explained in our packet. It looks like a typical ballroom setup. People are dancing, chatting at the bar, and sitting around small tables on large sofas.

We glance at each other with nervous smiles. I take his hand. "Let's head to the bar and get this wine opened." Walking though the ballroom toward the bar, I take in the scene. It is a medium-sized room with a marble dance floor in the middle. There are several people dancing to the romantic jazz music playing from the speakers surrounding the room. It looks very normal but feels weird; I sure hope a glass of wine helps shake the nerves.

Once we have our glasses in hand, we turn to walk away as a couple approaches us in conversation. The couple is a very attractive couple, and they appear to be in their mid-fifties. Her dress is exquisite. She is tall and thin with long flowing blonde hair and a beautiful diamond-encrusted mask. Her gown is a black-sequined gown with a plunging neckline. The dress is fitted to her fit body, and she is covered in excessive amounts of diamond jewelry.

He's tall and attractive in a Richard Gere sort of way. With a square jaw line, defined cheekbones, and silver hair with a slight curl to it, he's very sexy standing tall in a grey tuxedo with a silver mask. Looking around, I notice every man I see is in black; he's the only one in grey with the persona of wanting to stand out.

The idea of the masks is strange and wonderful at the same time. It's strange that you have no idea what people look like and who they are, but wonderful because they can't see who you are either.

The couple has introduced themselves as Susan and Edward. We reply with our fist names only as well, and they take the lead and direct the conversation. Edward starts speaking with Grant in the typical get to know you way. "What type of work do you do?" and "Are you from the New Orleans area?" They continue to chat, but I can no longer hear them over the music and Susan.

She has started the conversation by asking me if this is our first visit to "The Closet?" Assuming that is the nickname for the club, I give an embarrassed laugh with my eyes down and nod my head yes. She pulls me closer to her by my elbow. "There's nothing to be embarrassed about. We have been coming here for twenty years and we love it. No one will push you to do anything you're uncomfortable with. But I do urge you to push your limits get the full experience. We're not swingers; we simply enjoy watching and being watched. For us, it's a sexual high just to be in the atmosphere upstairs. I would prefer mixing it up with the ladies a bit, but it's no longer Edward's cup of tea.

Keep an open mind; this is like nothing you've ever experienced before. Have a drink or two down here, dance with your husband, and get comfortable. When ya'll are feeling a little frisky, come upstairs and see what is going on. If you don't enjoy it, you can always come back down to the vanilla party." She says that with a sour face and a wave of her hand. She turns, gives me a wink, grabs her husband's hand, and pulls him toward the stairs.

Edward looks back at Grant. "Hope to see ya'll upstairs soon." Grant takes my hand, puts our empty glasses down on the bar, and leads me to the dance floor. Pulling me close with one hand around my waist, his other hand is in mine as I wrap my free arm under his. I rest my cheek on his chest. We are molded together as one swaying along with the music.

We dance silently for a few songs. Listening to his breath and his heartbeat, it's loud and rapid. I look up at him just as he looks down at me with a smile. "What are you thinking my Bossy Girl? You want to mingle more down here, or do you want to go see what's going on upstairs?"

"I think we should grab a drink for the journey and head upstairs." Hand-in-hand, we walk over to the bar and order our drinks. As I reach for mine, I feel a woman's hand brush across my bare shoulder. When I turn, a woman immediately wraps me in a hug. Once I get my bearings, I see the red hair and know it's the woman from the doctor's office.

She has on a very large red ball gown. It's absolutely beautiful on her. The halter-top is crystal encrusted with a deep plunging back that extends right above the crack of her ass. The skirt is covered in layers and layers of red tulle.

"I'm glad to see you made it. I have been looking for you all night." Her hands slide down my shoulder to my wrist. Picking up my arm, a smile spreads across her face. She looks like the cat that ate the canary. Taking a step closer to me, she says, "I sure hope you plan on making use of that tonight. I have been dreaming of you ever since I first saw you."

Her warm breath hits my bare neck, and I get goose bumps. My heart races, and it's a strange feeling. I am a little turned on yet confused about my body's reaction. I feel as if it's betrayed me. The redhead does not introduce herself by name. Like everyone else here, a beautiful mask shields her, but I know it's the same woman from the doctor's office. She turns away and walks toward the stairs leading to all the action. When she's almost to the top, she turns and glances back over at us, blowing a kiss over her shoulder.

I look toward Grant trying to read his expression, but this time, his eyes give nothing away; a blank stare is all I see. I'm not sure how to read that. I pull him close to ask if he's ready to go up, but before I can get the words out, he grabs me firmly by the shoulders with a stern shake that startles me. I look up into his terror-filled eyes that look both scared and mad. "Are you okay? Grant? What's the matter? Did you change your mind? Do you want to go back to the hotel?" I watch his response closely as he takes a deep breath trying to compose himself.

"I don't want to share you! Not with a man and

not with a woman! You're mine and only mine. I don't even want people to see the parts of you that only I should see." Edward said a few things that really shook me, Shelby. He mentioned how we'll never be the same if we decide to share ourselves."

"I'm confused, Grant. Susan said they're not swingers. Let me in on where this is coming from."

"Edward started with general conversation, and when I said it was our first time, Edward noted you having a pink tag. He asked me a few more general questions about our plans, but not in an intrusive way. I shared with him where we might be headed. He cautioned me about the differences in seeing two girls on porn together and seeing your wife with another woman." He rubs his hand through his hair and takes another deep breath. "When that redheaded woman put her hands on you, she touched you like she wants to fuck you! I didn't like it, not at all. I know, I said this was my fantasy, but I really do believe some fantasies are better in your head; this is not something I want for us."

I open my arms to wrap Grant in a tight embrace and start to laugh. I can't stop. I pull back to see that Grant is a bit confused, and I try to calm myself in order to let him know that I'm relieved he feels that way. I truly want to be owned by him. I want him to be possessive of me, and most of all, I want him to treasure me.

"I'm thankful that the redhead showed up when she did. I'm also thankful she touched you the way she did, because after a few more drinks, we may have not been in the correct frame of mind to communicate this to each other."

We take a minute to sit at a table near the dance floor to regroup. We sit at that table for about thirty minutes cuddling and finishing our second glass of wine. I stand and take Grant's hand. "Lets go see what all the fuss is about. But first, let's hit the bar for a Sharpie to black out this pink." With a smile, Grant gets up and leads us to the bar where we do just that.

Chapter 21

We head up the narrow staircase, which brings us to the landing right outside the door. Another bouncer greets us asking us for our ID badges again. I am assuming this is to ensure someone doesn't sneak past the first bouncer. He also directs us to the dressing room and coat closet to leave our things.

I enter the dressing room to see a lady sitting there with a maid-like uniform. Just like the old fancy hotels, she's attending to the restroom making sure everyone has what they need. "Do you need help getting changed, ma'am?" Thank goodness she's here because I really didn't know how I was going to get out of this large skirt without falling over.

"Yes, ma'am, I do. Could you help me get out of this skirt without falling over?" Smiling warmly, she helps me and doesn't flinch when she sees the risqué outfit I have on underneath. I'm assuming this is a daily event for her. She hands me a tag and takes the skirt back to the coat closet. I freshen up my hair and makeup and step back to look at myself in the long mirror. My floor-length skirt is gone, and I'm left in my corset top and mini skirt that falls right below the roundness of my ass. The purple straps from my garter belt extend out from underneath the skirt clamping to my thigh-highs. It looks very sexy with these sky-high heels.

I step out of the dressing room to meet Grant. He looks even more handsome now that he's only half-dressed. The jacket and tie have been ditched, his shirtsleeves rolled up to his elbows, and his shirt is unbuttoned past his collarbone.

I take my claim tag and handkerchief out of my clutch and give it to Grant to carry in his pocket. The nice lady standing outside the door is waiting to take my clutch. She also asks for our masks; apparently, they are not allowed in the playroom. I must have skimmed over that piece of information in the booklet. Oh well, there's no turning back now.

We are off to the playroom, and I take a deep breath as Grant squeezes my hand and nods reassuringly. We enter the room, and it's very different from the room downstairs. There's club music playing loudly. The lights are dimmer and the room is separated into sections that have direct light over each area.

We walk through the room to see what's going on. As we proceed through the room, directly to our right are several sofas with pillows all over the place. There's a large portrait on the wall above this area that shows a very muscular man with dress slacks and no shirt. His pants appear to be unzipped, and a very sexy woman is between his legs giving him a blowjob. You can't see her face; you just see her perfect ass barley covered in a thong, breasts resting on his legs.

Looking down from the portrait, it appears everyone in this area is either giving or receiving oral sex. We pause and watch for a moment. There's a couple that mimics the portrait identically. He's sitting in an armless chair with his shirt off. His chest is chiseled to perfection, but you can tell he's not in his twenties. My eyes travel a little further down to see his grey trousers. Yep, it's Edward and Susan. She's kneeling on a pillow in between his legs. Her head comes up and down off of his cock, which allows us to see all of him. You can see his dick glistening in the dim candlelit room. There are candles on the wall and on most table surfaces.

Susan sees us watching them and removes her mouth to pump him with her hand. She locks her eyes on me and gives me a better view of his large cock. She strokes him slowly and seductively, as her eyes never leave mine. She then dips her head slightly to tease his slit with her tongue. She's watching us as we watch her. This is very intense, like watching a movie.

She gives us a smile and goes back to sucking him. There is another couple in this group of chairs and sofas. The woman is sitting up against the arm of the sofa with one leg pulled up and resting on the back of the sofa. The other leg is on the floor bracing herself, and both legs are covered in silky black thigh-highs. The thigh-highs are attached to a black lace garter belt around her waist. She has on a black bra with the middle cut out so her nipples are exposed and long black satin gloves that go past her elbows. She is using her satin covered fingers to roll one of her nipples as the man in between her legs licks her slowly. It appears no one here is in a rush to get off enjoying watching and being watched. Their eyes are wide open with pleasure and no shame as they are being observed.

I think we have fallen into their trap. Grant moves very close to me. I can hear and feel his breathing on the back of my neck along with his rock-hard cock pressing against the top of my ass. We watch her roll her nipples while the man sucks her clit, and I almost moan out loud myself from the scene. This is so carnal, so exposed, so wrong, yet we can't look away. Her legs are wide as he puts a finger into her slowly pumping it in and out while suckling her clit. She starts to arch her back and moan in pleasure as he adds another finger. My heartbeat is starting to race along with my breathing. The scene is so oddly beautiful. They are so open to each other and anyone else watching. I notice both of their tags on their bracelets are black as he continues to pump in and out of her. Her bracelet shines in the candlelight as she lowers her hand to run it though his hair. Their pace is more hurried now, and she has started to shake and scream through her orgasm. I'm not sure we will make it to the back of this room without making love to each other right here on the floor.

Grant guides me to the rear of the club where we come across the last section of sofas before the line of sheer-covered beds. This area is full of people. I have never seen an orgy before, but this must be what it looks like. Everyone is touching someone and being touched by someone else. I immediately see the redhead. She's laying on her back with another woman in between her legs. She has her fingers on her own clit making circles while the other woman licks her. The other woman has her rear in the air and is being fucked from behind by a man.

There's a little too much going on in that section for me, and we continue further into the club. We see the lined up beds shielded with sheer white fabric. Some beds have the fabric pulled open, and this appears to be an invitation to anyone that wants to join. Others have the fabric pulled shut just to be viewed, not entered.

Grant pushes me up against the wall nearest the first bed and starts to kiss me fiercely. It's rough and possessive. His hands are all over me, up my bodice, over the swells of my breasts, and up the back of my neck. He puts his hand in my hair, pulling my head back firmly, kissing my jaw and down the front of my throat and over my chest.

"I want to fuck you so badly right now, Shelby, but I don't want to be on display. What we have is for us. I don't want to show them our love. Let's find the locked rooms the brochure talked about."

We hustle down the long corridor past the exposed beds to find all the doors wide open. Not one of the rooms are in use! "This is a sign that this place is not for us; it's erotic, but once is enough, don't you agree?"

I nod my head yes as we are the only couple in this place that can't screw each other in front of an audience. "Enough with all this chit-chat, Grant, come fuck me," I say as I pull him into the room.

"Always, my Bossy Girl!" He does as he's told, and he does it quick. He doesn't remove a shred of my clothing. Picking me up swiftly, he lays me across the bed and heads back to the door to lock it. Walking back from the door, he unzips his pants. Once he reaches me, he turns me over and pushes my shoulders down on the bed.

He enters me with force and pounds quickly. It feels so sexy for him to be so dominant. It takes him a moment to regain control of himself to give me steady thrusts. I am now able to rock back and forth on my knees to meet him. My skirt is pushed up high on my waist, with my breasts spilling out of my corset. Grant's hands are firm on my hips pulling me back and forth. I love when he pulls all the way out letting me feel his entire length.

Slowing his motions, I feel his cock grow larger. I feel the walls of my pussy contract onto him as my orgasm comes over me in a pulsating wave. It literally starts in my toes and moves through my entire body all the way up to my head. He slows down just enough to let me catch my breath, but does not stop thrusting, making it that much better.

After passionately rolling around in the bed for a few minutes, I'm able to get on top of him, and I brace my arms on the headboard behind his head. His green eyes stare up at me. Using the headboard for support, I ride him with force and depth. I am so wet, my slickness allows my clit to rub on his pelvis. I feel my orgasm coming again so soon, and I want Grant to come with me. "Do you like my soaking wet pussy on you? Do you want me to fuck you harder?" He gets so turned on by dirty talk, and right on cue, we both come together with fireworks. I ride him slowly until I no longer feel him pulsating inside of me. I collapse on top of him as he wraps his arms around me, flipping us over and devouring me in kisses.

"I never thought it was possible to love you more than I did five months ago. Thank you for going out of your comfort zone for us; thank you for letting me take you in this room and not exploiting our love out there. Come on, Bossy Girl, let's get the hell out of here."

I use the handkerchief in Grant's pocket to clean up. We hurry though the playroom hand-in-hand with no concern to our surroundings. It was an erotic experience, but I don't think we will find ourselves here again.

    We ring in the New Year in each other's arms alone together and in love back at the hotel.

Epilogue

We are still on a sexual high that's now our relationship. We both have made a constant effort to feed each other's needs, and it has been absolutely awesome. Going to Savannah's Closets was a wild experience; however, once in a lifetime was good enough for us. We have stuck to the discreet foreplay in public with wild nights at home. We've made a vow to rent a limo every year for a ride over the lake and back on our anniversary.

While our relationship has been great, things have been bumpy for Samantha. She lost her Great-Aunt Gertrude, which was expected, but it wasn't easy for her. Tragically, she also lost her husband. Phillip was a mechanic on an offshore oilrig. He was being evacuated from the rig during a storm, and the helicopter went down in the Gulf of Mexico. Grant and I have been trying to push her to keep busy with her Aunt's dream of re-opening the Burlesque Club, but I'm not sure we will be able to pull her out from her new commitment to never be in a relationship again.

From The Author

I hope you enjoyed Grant and Shelby's journey. I started reading what I lovingly call smut a few short years ago and said, "I can do that, and I can do it with a hometown New Orleans flair!" And with that, Shelby and Grant were created. My wonderful husband encouraged me to write and share with my fellow smut-reading friends. It was their positive reaction that pushed me to publish my dirty thoughts.

Please tell me what you think of my book by leaving a review on Amazon or sending me an email to mailto:msmonicamay@gmail.com

LIKE my Facebook page to get updates on The New Orleans Temptation Series Book 2.

https://www.facebookcom/pages/Monica-May